TWISTS OF FATE

The BEWITCHED Trilogy
Book 3

KELLY ALLEYN

blackbird

First Published in 2024 by Blackbird Digital Books
Blackbird Digital Books
Copyright Kelly Alleyn 2024
ISBN: 978-1-0686505-2-9
The moral right of the author has been asserted

http://blackbird-books.com/

Contents

Prologue

Hawk Bay City Herald

Tragedy at the Tower

Following the unexplained explosion of the Tower, two colleagues from the popular TV station that broadcasts The Bitch's Hour are presumed dead.

Fragmentary remains have been removed from the ashes and taken to the forensics laboratory, who say that identification may prove impossible due to the intense heat to which they were submitted.

Known to be missing are TV presenter Decima Gauld, Josh Harris the special effects wizard, and a cleaner named as Marla Carrera. It is feared that all lost their lives. 41 people who were in the Tower at the time of the explosion have been accounted for. Two are in critical condition and several others have sustained non-life-threatening injuries.

1

Fugitive

Decima

Four days ago I was a high-flying TV presenter. I wore designer clothes and lived in a five-million-dollar house.

Now here I am with most of my hair burned off, wearing Alice's clothes that are three sizes too big, hiding in a weird house out in the boondocks and presumed dead.

The events of the night of the explosion are still hazy. Images flash in and out but they are too vague. I know it happened because of the burns on my body, but I can't figure out how Alice and I got out of there and arrived at Alice's house.

Apparently I slept for two days.

I woke up when I heard Cory's voice. I fumbled out of bed to find my way downstairs and heard Sean talking. My world fell apart when I heard him say Josh, my big bearlike lover, was dead and that the Tower had been deliberately blown up. It confirmed all my fears – somebody was trying to kill me. I screamed and stumbled down the stairs.

All hell was let loose. Cory caught me just before I fell. Alice's mother came out of the lounge dressed in what looked like a beekeepers' outfit. She locked the door behind her shouting what the hell was going on. The hall filled with a putrid smell that seemed to come from under the door of the lounge.

Cory and Alice led me into the kitchen and sat me down. Sean was there flapping his hands up and down. He and Cory were both angry with Alice for not telling them I was safe. She explained that it's believed there was an attempt on my life; they want whoever is responsible to think I'm dead, and nobody would think to look for me here.

She and her parents are just trying to protect me. Which, really, is more than I deserve after the way I've treated Alice. Where else could I go, anyway? I have no friends.

Why do I have the feeling that my father is behind this? Why try to kill me if I'm the goose that lays the golden eggs he needs?

We've all agreed that, for my safety, we will, for now, continue to let people believe I am dead.

Cory will look after Twinkle and Barney until I'm able to come out of hiding. I didn't even ask how he got them, but I knew he'd look after them well.

As soon as they've gone, I go straight back to the small room where I sleep. There's only one bed, so I suppose Alice is sleeping in the two chairs pushed together. There is so much I need to know, but I'm too tired to care at the moment. Knowing my dogs are safe is everything to me. Anything else can wait.

I catch sight of myself in the mirror. My hair! Where is my hair? It looks like a brush that just came down a chimney, black spikes sticking up in every direction. And the skin on my face is red and wrinkled. It burns when I touch it. I throw myself onto the bed and scream and scream and scream.

A hand touches my shoulder. 'It's OK Decima. Everything will be OK.'

Alice sits on the side of the bed holding a bowl of something that stinks like old fish.

'I'm just going to put a little of this on your burns. It will make them heal quickly.'

'No!' I gag and push the bowl away.

'Yes,' she says. 'Yes. Keep still.'

She smears it all over my face.

'There. Now your arms.'

She rubs the horrible gloop all over my arms. Before my eyes, as if by magic, my skin returns to normal.

I get off the bed and look in the mirror. My face has completely healed.

'What is that stuff?'

'Something my mother makes.'

She holds up a cup to my face.

'Drink.'

I sip it. It tastes like a strange mixture of herbs and something sweet.

'What is she, some kind of witch?'

'Yes,' says Alice. 'She's a witch. So am I. Go to sleep now.'

My eyes suddenly feel very, very heavy.

2

Where am I?

Decima

I drift off. When I wake up, Alice is still there. Watching over me like a blue-eyed Angel of Death.

I try to take it all in. Alice. A witch. Her mother, a witch. This house, a witch's house. That thick musty but minty smell that fills this room? The smell of witch.

'Josh? Is he really…?'

Her face clouds. 'He didn't stand a chance.'

'It was meant for me wasn't it,' I whisper. 'I'm the one who's meant to be dead.'

'We don't know that. We know nothing for sure.'

I move to get up but there's a sharp stab in my throat, a raw pain like the skin is being scraped off from the inside of my neck.

'Rest now. You're all cuts and bruises, Decima. Nothing more. You will recover but you must do as we say. We were both very lucky.'

A fresh wave of horror sweeps over me. 'Digby? Where's Digby!'

'He's right here, Decima, waiting for you – here.'

I snatch my bear and hold him close.

'I didn't want you to squash him in your sleep. He's fragile after his ordeal.'

At the touch of his fur, my shoulders drop and my breathing steadies. Alice may be a witch, but she understands my relationship with Digby.

'Er, I have to tell you, the books, your first edition collection in the Tower…'

'Gone?'

She nods.

'Jane Austen,' I groan. 'Signed.'

'They'll have been insured.'

'It was a fake, Alice. They were all fakes, gifts from my 'loving' father who now wants me dead. So good riddance.'

'That's the spirit. Look here. Cory has brought some books over from your house.' She picks up a Steffanie Holmes from a pile of paperbacks. 'I'll read to you now if you like. You settle back and…'

'I've read it. How did Cory get the dogs?'

'He picked up the keys from your handyman.'

'Grant? So much for security.'

'What would you like me to read to you? What *haven't* you read?'

I look around the tiny box bedroom. Stuck above a cheap pine dressing table cluttered with plants, is an old Scorpio poster, curling at the corners.

'So this is your room?'

'It was, yes. You know how sentimental parents can be about their grown kids' stuff.'

'Why all the plants? They stink.'

'They're herbs, Decima, to help you heal. Don't speak too loudly, they hear every word.'

I take a long hard look into her trusting blue eyes. 'I have to go home.'

I reach out for my phone. 'Grant and the boys will get me what I need…'

I run my hand over the side-table. 'What's THIS?' I pick up a dusty black screen smeared in fingerprints. 'Where's my phone?'

'I'm afraid it was destroyed, Decima. This is one of my old ones. We've put a SIM in. Not in your name.'

'Since when do you have permission to take over my life, Alice? I have to go home. I'm quite capable of protecting myself. I've looked after myself for long enough haven't I? Even without all this, this… family vibe going on.'

'You *can't* go home, Decima. You're *dead.*'

'What?'

'We told you, remember? Oh dear. Look, you're still very fragile. And think about it for a moment, you were certain that somebody or something was trying to kill you, right? So please, please rest here and get your strength back. Let the dust settle. Your father is on his way.'

I start. 'Here?'

'Not *here* here. At least I hope not. He's flying in to give a press conference at the City Hall this evening. We'll watch the livestream. He thinks you're dead too Decima.'

I smile to myself. 'Well, that's interesting!'

I wonder what he'll say? He'll be genuinely sad. For himself. For Josh. Losing his right-hand man will hit him right where it hurts. But me?

I flick through the screen.

'I've loaded some of your favorite Apps. It all works fine. Just for now. Until… until… well, until this is all sorted out.'

'Uber? Where's freaking Uber?'

'Sorry. We can't leave anything to chance, Decima. It's to protect you. That's all it is, I promise.'

I open WhatsApp. It's empty.

'Where's WhatsApp? Where is everybody?'

Alice is shaking her head.

'Too risky for me is it?'

'Twitter is there!' she says brightly. 'I mean X or whatever it's called. We've signed you in under a fake name so you can play with that as much as you like. As long as you're cautious.'

'My boys. Cory, how do I reach Cory? Sean? Ramon? Josh? Oh Josh, I can't believe it. Is Ramon OK? Where is he?'

'Sean is here helping out. Ramon is in Korea, Shooting

his film. A big feature. At least that's some good news.'

'Good for Ramon. Not for me. I'll miss him.' I scroll through the phone and click through to Twitter.

Macabre isn't the word. Not many people get to read their own obituaries. #RIPDecima is trending. Everybody is posting really nice things about me. Even Lorelei Thornheart's witch posse, my old #1 enemy's supporters.

'Look at this,' I hand the phone to Alice.

'Aww Lorelei, how sweet of her.'

'Sweet! Read it out.'

Lorelei Thornheart @loreleithorn99 'We never saw eye to eye, but Decima was a one-off. There was nobody else who could have taken over my show with such style.'

'*Her* show? Her her *her*, it's all about her. Even for RIP Decima, you can read *HaHa I won, Lorelei*.'

'She's a kind person, Decima. She always was…'

'I suppose she's a *real* witch too is she?'

The way Alice looks at me gives it away.

'You're everywhere aren't you?'

My online spats with Lorelei over whether she is a real or a fake witch go back a long way. Clickbait for both of us. She first faked a ghost interview on *The Witch's Hour*, the CGO TV show I took over. Josh's special effects were so convincing that millions were taken in and she went viral. When she was exposed and fired, I got my big presenting break. Much to her fury we changed the title of the show to *The Bitch's Hour* and got a massive sponsorship deal. She set up her own YouTube ghost interview channel, pulling in millions of hits. Our fight became a public battle for everybody to pile in on.

'She's having the last laugh. I don't like it. I don't like it at all.'

'She's not,' says Alice. 'She's in a worse situation than you right now.'

'What's worse than dead?'

'Jail? Her #ghostfake situation has peaked. Like, bad peak.'

'#Ghostfake! So there's a tag?'

'Her church has folded, she's being sued all over the place, apparently. I'm surprised she's not in jail already.'

'Well that is good news. Oh look, here's another one:

Lorelei Thornheart @loreleithorn99 I miss my friend. Heart emoji, broken heart emoji…

'Lies lies and more lies.' I scroll back through her timeline. 'I'm tempted to reply, Alice. Message her from beyond the grave. Decima here. Pitching to be your next ghost guest? Ha ha. That'd freak her right out.'

Alice giggles. 'Go ahead. She won't know it's really you. She'll think you're a troll. I'll get you some coffee.'

3

Strange house

Sean

This house is some kind of crazy. Like something from an old TV series. The garden swallows it up with climbing plants all around the windows and on right up to the roof. The hallway is stacked with packing crates. It's all higgledy piggledy. Doors and stairs everywhere you look. There's a door on the right that's always locked, what's that about? It seems the kitchen, which runs the full length of the house, is where they hang out. A desk at one end is in danger of collapsing beneath stacks of paper and pots of paint. The long pine table in the center is heaped with bunches of herbs, jars of paste, cakes cooling on racks, half-empty cups of coffee, gardening magazines. A row of old dressers cover one wall. Nobody around here is houseproud that's for sure.

Alice's mother points to a chair. 'Have a seat, Sean. I'll make some coffee. Now I don't want you to get this wrong. We think the world of you, we really do. You are so good for Alice. You'll make a great couple.'

I can feel a 'but' on the way. She sweeps a pile of magazines to one side and puts a mug in front of me.

'The thing is, this house only has two bedrooms. We don't have any guestrooms. So you can't stay here I'm afraid. Decima is already in Alice's room and Alice is sleeping on a chair. I am really sorry.'

'I'll sleep on the porch then. I'm not leaving Alice until I know she's safe. And anyways, I don't have any money for my rent. So as long as you don't mind, I'm happy to sleep outside.'

'Don't be silly,' says Alice. 'You can't sleep outside. We can make some space in the garden shed, can't we?'

'I suppose so. It's not ideal, but if Sean doesn't mind. And naturally he will eat with us in the house, he's almost one of the family.'

I'd sleep on a pile of rocks to stay close to Alice, or on a heap of burning coals. I'm not going to let any harm come to her.

We soon turn the garden shed into a really cool space. Alice sweeps it and I tidy up the pots and buckets and wipe down the window. There's a small washroom attached, so it has all I need. It's kind of cozy. I could imagine being cuddled up in here, with Alice.

We bring in a lounger and some cushions to make a bed and Alice finds a small table from somewhere in the house. There's electricity for my phone and music. It's all I need. I even like the scent of the compost bags heaped up under the shelf.

The house is, as I said, weird, but Alice's folk are so chilled out and have made me feel at home, so I'm full on relaxed with them. The garden is a dream, an organized jungle of colors that creep and blend into each other like a kaleidoscope and wrap themselves around the house like a protective blanket. The scent is out of this world. So romantic. It would be a perfect place for a wedding.

4

The truth comes out

Alice

It feels strange having people in the house. The only visitors I can remember are the journalist Rex Tillman, who came after my mother's garden was trashed, but he didn't come into the house, and Jai when he came for lunch. We are not like other people, we never have been. I saw how Cory and Sean looked around as if they couldn't believe what they were seeing. I've seen homes on TV where everything is in its place but ours is the opposite.

Until now I've never really thought about our lifestyle and how we live. It's always been like that. Peaceful, mother with her garden and screechers, my father either out at work or in his studio with his art. Funny, when I realize just how different we are.

How many families actually have a friend living in a shed in the garden? How many women have to sleep curled up on chairs because somebody else is in their bed?

I check regularly on Decima. She's in a deep healing sleep and that suits me very well, because once she wakes up properly there's going to be a lot of explaining to do. On top of that, I can't imagine how she'll react to living in a place like this, so different from her own luxurious home. Whether she likes it or not, she's going to have to stay here until we know she's safe.

Just before 6.00 pm I wake her to go downstairs and gather around Sean's pride and joy, his Samsung Galaxy Z Fold with its extra-large screen, to watch the press conference. Gauld stands in front of the ruins of the Tower trying to look sorrowful. At his side, Decima's sister Ornella taps him mindlessly on his arm.

'A tragic tragedy,' he splutters. 'Everything gone, just boom.' He throws his hands up in the air. 'My magnificent achievement, a monument to my life's work, all fallen down. Down. An accident nobody could have foreseen.'

'Rubbish,' says my father. 'That was no accident. The place was blown up.'

His firm of engineers is working with the forensic teams to establish the cause of the explosion. It's very early days and will take time to uncover the truth but they have already found proof that it was deliberate.

'He was trying to kill me,' Decima whispers.

'So there's no indication at this point of what caused the explosion?'

Gauld hangs his head, shaking it slowly from side to side. Ornella bites her lip.

'What are your plans,' asks a voice from the crowd.

The camera focuses on a man wearing an eye-patch who seems vaguely familiar.

'Do you intend to rebuild?'

'I will start work as soon as the insurance money comes in. I'll rebuild bigger and better.'

'Can you tell us how much the building was insured for?'

Ornella pipes up: 'Don't forget the inshuwance for Decima, too, Daddy.'

Gauld turns and glares at her.

'Nothing could compensate for the loss of my d… beloved daughter. I cannot bear to talk about it. A beautiful, talented young woman, at the top of her game, earning the station millions. She is irreplaceable. Decima was devoted to me and my greatest pride and joy.'

Ornella scowls as he manufactures a sob.

'I realize this is a most painful time for you, so forgive me if I'm being insensitive, but may I ask if the remains have now been identified? Are you certain that your daughter was in the Tower at the time of the explosion?'

It's the man with the eye-patch, who I recognise now as the journalist who came to investigate after Astrid's garden was destroyed. He's working on a Netflix documentary about Gauld's shady business empire. Just after he came to see the damage done to my mother's garden he was mugged and so badly beaten he lost an eye.

Gauld wipes away invisible tears. 'I understand that the condition of the, the remains,' he holds back a fake sob, 'is such that identification may be impossible but I know, deep in my heart I know that Decima is gone. A part of me has died. It feels as if I have lost a limb. Nothing and nobody will ever replace her.'

Ornella scowls, and says: 'You said I ...'

'Ouch! ' she squeals as he kicks her on the ankle.

Gauld wraps a fat arm around her and pulls her towards him.

'My poor baby,' he croons, 'this has been a terrible shock to her, losing her sister. They were very close.' He turns her face into his chest and squeezes it hard.

A hand pops up from the crowd.

'Mr Gauld, I believe one of your technicians may also have been a victim. Has there been any word from the special effects guy?'

'Josh, you mean? No, there's been no news of him. At this stage we have to assume that tragically he and my daughter have both perished and will be impossible to replace. We do not know why either of them would have been in the Tower at that time of night. And now, if you will excuse me, I need to be alone.'

He lumbers out of shot with Ornella trotting along beside him.

'Bastard,' says Decima. 'I've only ever been a source of income for him. He's a vile, greedy monster. He'll be raking in all the insurance money as fast as he can.'

'He's not your real father, is he?' asks Patrick.

'Godfather. My parents died in a fire. Then he adopted me and my sister and got control of our inheritance. Now he's going to collect millions in insurance. That's his game. He's done it before. He'll do it again. It's no coincidence at all.'

Cory, who has been watching in silence, says quietly,

'It's obvious, Decima is in real danger. If he learns she's alive, he'll be looking for her to finish the job. We have to find somewhere to keep her safe.'

'Decima is staying here. With us,' says my father. 'She'll be safe here.'

'Could you please not talk about me as if I'm not here. I'm not quite dead yet!'

'Yes, that's right,' my mother says, ignoring her. 'Nobody will think of looking here. We'll take care of her.'

'But…'

'No buts, young lady. You are staying with us until you are no longer in danger. No argument.'

'But where will I sleep? It's kind of Alice but I need my own bed. My special mattress, my Egyptian bed linen. And I must have my en suite.'

'You must,' my father says soothingly, 'and you will be back under your own roof just as soon as we are satisfied that you are out of danger.'

'Exactly,' adds my mother.

'I'll be going back to my place in a few days,' I say, 'so you'll have the whole room to yourself.'

Sean jumps up. 'I'll come with you, Alice. To look after you.'

My mother sees the expression on my face and says, 'Sean dear, I was hoping you would stay with us for a while, to give me a hand. You're one of the family now and I could really do with some help with the garden.'

For a moment he looks crestfallen, then he brightens up.

'Thank you, Mrs Archer, I'd be delighted..."

He stops in mid-sentence as something flies in through the door and perches on the back of a chair.

'Tum de dum,' chirps Zylch. 'Free blind mice.'

Decima shrieks. 'What on earth is that?'

Zylch folds his wings away, tilts his head on one side and blinks endearingly a few times.

Cory and Sean jump up from their seats and stare at Zylch as he hops onto the table towards Decima, who is paralyzed with horror.

I scoop him into my arms. 'His name is Zylch. He's a screecher.'

'I thought it was your cat?' says Sean.

'He can be a cat. He can be anything he wants to be, can't you Zylch?'

'Yes, I can be little mouse,' he transforms into a mouse and sits on my shoulder, smoothing his whiskers.

Decima screams louder.

'Be something cute,' I tell him.

'Snake?' he says.

'No!' Decima shuffles her chair away as far as she can.

'Snake is beautiful, but it isn't really cute, Zylch. How about puppy?'

He shakes himself and jumps to the ground. A fluffy poodle puppy with neon blue fur waddles over to Decima, wagging his tail.

'Goodness me,' says Cory. 'I've never seen anything like that. How is it operated – remote control? Bluetooth? It's extraordinary.'

'It's not a toy,' I say.

'Well then, what exactly is it?'

'Will dinner be ready for 7.00?' asks my father.

'Yes, dear. You are staying to eat with us too,' she nods at Cory. 'Alice, explain about Zylch.'

I take a deep breath. 'I think by now you must all realize we are not a 'normal' family.'

A knowing look passes between Sean and Cory while Decima stares at me with her mouth hanging open. I'm trying to think how to begin. The only way is to jump right in.

'As I told you the other day, Decima. Though I'm not sure you believed me. My mother is a witch.'

They all turn to look at my plump little mother with her frizzy hair and button nose. She doesn't look anything out of the ordinary, unless you peer closely through her small gold-rimmed glasses and notice that her eyes are a strange ice blue.

'Alice!' Cory says angrily.

Astrid turns from the pot she's stirring on the stove, and smiles.

'Her mother was a witch, her mother before her, right back through the ages. It's passed down the female line. I am also a witch.'

Cory clears his throat and coughs nervously.

My mother opens the crockery cupboard and takes out six plates. Still smiling, she picks up one and aims it at the table. It floats slowly through the air and settles neatly, silently, on the table. She repeats it with another five plates, and then the knives and forks and glasses all in similar fashion. They arrange themselves perfectly while Astrid continues stirring.

Sean mutters to nobody in particular, 'I knew it. I always knew it.'

Cory wipes a hand over his eyes and shakes his head. 'So it's really true.'

'I need a drink,' says Decima. 'Do you have any champagne?'

5

A favor from Alice

Cory

Most assume that twins are closer than close. Siblings with the volume turned high. But for Jonty and I it's the opposite. My escape to the US to try my luck as a basketball pro was the perfect solution for us both. He was welcome to the title and all the headaches that went with owning that enormous pile of soggy old bricks with freezing bathrooms and tepid water – the best the cranky old boiler could produce. I could go on – the list is endless, not least the staff who never stayed long because of Jonty's monstrous behavior.

So when I heard about his tumble at polo, I had no idea that he was at death's door. I wouldn't have known he was in hospital at all if my old pal Simon, the bar manager of our local, The Sportsman, hadn't tracked me down on Facebook.

The messages became increasingly urgent. 'Come home' soon before it was 'too late'.

To be perfectly honest, my first thought was to

wonder if I truly needed to see him before he died. If that, indeed, was going to happen. Nobody's dead until they're dead, are they? More to the point, and what I kept on telling myself – in his last hours on earth, he'd get no joy from my presence.

Our personality types do merge in one respect: neither of us is the settling-down type. At CGO TV I had found all the stability, companionship and, to boot, variety and excitement, most guys can only dream of.

Internet dating was Jonty's thing. Hook-up apps provided an endless string of women who'd try and take him on despite all the nasty personal habits and bodily odors that went with excessive drinking. Add a heavy dose of arrogance, entitlement and arctic bathroom temperatures and you can begin to imagine why no woman would stay with him for any length of time. Which suited him fine.

Neither of us had any plans to settle down. I knew at least that when, if, he died, there would be no succession problems. There would be lawyers to legalize the Trust paperwork into my sole name rather than the two of us, that sort of thing. The headache of what next with the castle if Jonty wasn't there any more could be filed neatly into worries about things that hadn't happened yet and probably wouldn't happen for decades.

Then it all blew up at once. Jonty: at death's door. The Tower: gone. Josh: dead. Decima too, it was presumed at first.

When I discovered that she was alive, my elation took me by surprise. In that moment I realized how much I truly love Hawk Bay City and my CGO TV family, with, crucially, Decima at its heart. America is as much my true home as England is my past.

If Alice is suffering from the trauma of that awful night she doesn't show it. She and her parents care for Decima so well. Sean, too, is there doing all that he can to help. We're pulling together. All thoughts of Jonty's possible impending demise went on the back burner whilst I absorbed the shock and rallied round. A convenient excuse? Maybe. Though Decima's two stressed-out dogs Twinkle and Barney to care for were real enough.

It's funny how life takes an unexpected swerve sometimes, isn't it? I knew I had to come clean to Decima about my true identity and what was going on at home. She was furious, she's always cross about something or another, but this was off the scale. And oh, she is beautiful when angry.

If I was an aristocrat, I must be hiding great riches, was her first question. I put her right on that straight away. What income the trust fund and farming land provides is suckered straight back into the running costs of the estate, such as it is. The rest gets poured behind the snug bar of The Sportsman or gets spent on renting dodgy polo ponies too small for a man his size.

On the very morning after the fire, just as I'd

committed to feeding and walking Twinkle and Barney indefinitely, I got the dreaded message from the UK. 'Come at once'. It wasn't as simple as that, was it! Who else could take on the dogs? It wasn't only the Tower we lost that night. Our entire CGO family is in pieces.

I go to our old *Decima's Guys* WhatsApp group. Just seeing our names together Josh; Cory; Sean; Ramon… makes me want to weep.

There aren't many messages there from before the fire. We saw each other every day at the studios so there wasn't much need for it. Just rendezvous stuff. Macabre, but I do scroll through, pausing at Josh's messages. It's still impossible to believe that he's gone. I don't think I will even start to understand it until his body has been found and identified. If that ever happens.

And then there's Ramon.

Ramon, Ramon. Life hey? It gives, it takes away, it gives. The dice has fallen the other way for Ramon. A simple Mexican boy who dreamed of becoming a film star is, right now, living the dream.

He was plucked from our midst by one of Decima's studio guests, Michiko Kim, the Korean movie producer. Before we knew it he'd been whisked off to Halluywood. Yes you heard that correctly. Halluywood is the Korean version of Hollywood. Michiko Kim's films have bigger budgets and bigger audiences than all the Hollywood franchises put together.

A thought strikes me. Will he have heard the news?

It's a local issue and no way international. Unless he's sought out our news? I'm sure he's way too busy for that… He might be homesick, though? But if he had heard he'd have been in touch by now.

I twirl my phone in my hand. What to say? How to break it to him?

I open up a dialogue and type.

Hey…

The dots immediately start jumping around… He's typing… My throat constricts. How am I going to say this?

Hey, man, how's yourself?

I sigh, it's Sean. I call him and explain I'm about to break the news. When I return to WhatsApp Ramon has replied.

Heya guys. How's it going?

Here goes:

Prepare yourself, Ramon. There's been a terrible accident… at the Tower. Burnt to the ground.

NO?

Yep.

Everyone OK?

I take a deep breath and explain briefly.

That's unbelievable. Josh? JOSH? You sure?

His body hasn't been found yet but he was definitely in there. The night watchman saw him going in an hour before the fire broke out.

There's more to this, Ramon…

There's a long pause. A welcome pause that gives me a moment to gather my thoughts. I give him as long as he needs to absorb the news. What do I say about Decima? Would any cyber security trolls really be monitoring our little WhatsApp group? Am I being too paranoid in not spelling it out here? Before he googles it, I must let him know that she is alive.

Listen, are you free now? Quick chat?

My phone buzzes and I go straight in.

'Hey listen carefully. The reports say that Decima is dead, OK. But she's fine. She's in hiding, because it looks very much like this was an attempt on her life.'

There's a long pause while he takes it in.

'Ah OK,' he says eventually. 'Well that's something. So Gauld really was trying to bump her off? What about Alice? Sean?'

'All is very well with the love birds. I think you knew that? How's it all going for you there, man?

'Unbelievable. Like landing on another planet.'

'And the film?'

'The film's going well. Wow, man, that's a lot to take in. Thanks for the flags-up, I'd have freaked if I'd found that news online. We're shooting right now, it's so full on I don't get any time to go on my phone much. But we're at this supercool Buddhist temple. You'd die Cory, you'd love it here. And the women, let me tell you about Korean girls…'

'I'm glad you've made yourself at home,' I laugh.

'Western guys, they love us!'

'You got friends there?'

'No, but let's just say plenty of company if I ever need it.'

'What about the language?

'They all speak English. Everybody in the film world. I stay in downtown Seoul when we're not on location. I have to speak Korean for the movie, but that's a line by line thing. I don't have a clue what I'm sayin' but I'm making the right noises. I think.'

'You're looking amazing, I'm sure.'

'Pretty neat in this ancient nobleman garb let me tell you. I got a sword! There's a lot of fighting.'

'You'd be good at that.'

'Yeah man, I'm winning here. But I'm, well, I can't believe what you said. You OK?'

'Getting through it.'

I wind up the conversation without going into my own dramas. He has enough news to take in as it is.

We say our goodbyes and I promise to keep him updated, even if he can't respond too often.

My next problem is the dogs. I've been staying at Decima's to look after them but now I need to get to England pronto.

Decima's handyman Grant, isn't much help. I gather he's scared of them, especially Twinkle, the little terrier. I can never understand that in people.

Fortunately, I'd already confided my situation back in

England to Sean. He's had time to absorb and accept that I wasn't who he thought I was. I call him back on the off-chance that he might be able to squeeze in some dog care and he comes up with a solution right away. One that I'd never, ever have thought of in a million years.

When Sean had gone on and on at me about his trip to the stars with Alice, I'd naturally assumed I was witnessing the imagination of a man deeply in love. Helped, I didn't doubt, by a few drugs here and there. At the time, I was suffering badly. I could barely listen to Sean's joyful tales of time spent with the girl I had set my own heart on. Now, thank goodness, my own feelings for Alice are those of pure friendship. As soon as I realized how right they are for each other, Cupid did me a favor and flew off to bother somebody else.

Now, with logic thankfully returned to me, another set of crazy thoughts have taken over. As Alice truly is a witch, from a wicca dynasty no less, what if she had literally flown him? What if it hadn't been one of Sean's druggy highs after all? What do you think? Yes, right. Crazy I know. But I have to find out if there's any substance to the claims.

What happened next is difficult to believe. Even for me. You see, Alice has this kind of quantum App on her phone. It's called **Brmstick.** It will take her anywhere she wants at the speed of light. Sean's trip to the stars, I'm being assured, really did happen.

I put it to her. Could she take me to the hospital to

see my dying brother? Just for a few hours, a moment even. The only way it could work was if she could take me there and back because of the dogs.

She explained that **Brmstick** didn't allow her to leave passengers behind anyway, so as long as I was OK with her accompanying me to the hospital, we were on.

6

Decima settling in

Alice

I've had to keep giving myself quite a few calming potions over the last three days. Decima has been very tiresome. I have to remember that she has had a terrible fright. All of us are doing everything we can to help her heal and keep her safe until we find out what is going on, but all she's done is complain.

Funnily enough my mother has been extremely patient with her, the most maternal I've ever known her. She's created a new recipe for a salve to heal Decima's face, and the scarring is almost invisible already. And the sweetest thing – she made a turban from a piece of purple fabric to cover Decima's head where the hair was burned off. She's even pinned fresh flowers to it. They really seem to be bonding.

Even stranger is the way Decima and my father are getting on like a house on fire. Oops, didn't mean to say that, it's all too recent. But you know what I mean, they really do hit it off. He seems genuinely fond of her, and she obviously respects him. He brought home a gift box of fresh fruit for her, and a bunch of flowers. Which is quite odd as the garden overflows with beautiful flowers that he could have picked. I raised an eyebrow when I saw the bouquet, and he said: 'I just want to cheer the poor girl up.'

Good thing I'm not the jealous type. It's a revelation seeing another side to my parents.

Now she's up and about, Decima's been wearing some of my old clothes which, as she pointed out, are three sizes too big for her. I must admit she looks really funny with the flowery headdress and the baggy tracksuits. I **Brmsticked** to her place last night and collected some of her clothes and beauty products, so she's looking a bit more cheerful now.

When she came to breakfast this morning and found Sean in the kitchen helping my mother, she snapped, 'What is *he* doing here?'

'Just like you, dear,' said my mother. 'Sean is staying with us for a little while, to give me a hand.'

'Huh.'

Sean hands her a cup of coffee which she sniffs suspiciously. She starts to say something, then takes the cup and nods to him. 'Thanks.'

'Sit yourself down now, Mrs Archer,' Sean says. 'I'll take care of breakfast. Let me do it.'

'You do ours, Sean, and I'll do Decima's.'

While he fries eggs and cooks waffles, my mother

chops and slices pineapple and mangoes for Decima. As I watch her, I'm reminded of the time Decima tricked me into interviewing Sita, and how Sita put me at ease when she mentioned mangoes. I feel a little pain in my heart. Will it ever go away?

'It's too kind of you,' says Decima when my mother puts the plate in front of her. 'But please don't go to any trouble for me. I'm happy to eat whatever you're having. I am so grateful for all you're doing for me.'

Then she bursts into tears and starts wailing. 'Josh! Josh is dead! I can't bear it, my beautiful bear. Dead.'

'There, there,' says my mother, patting her gently on her turban. 'We don't know that. There is no proof yet.'

'I can feel it. Josh would have been in contact if he were alive. He'd want to be with me. Sean and Cory too.'

'He could just be injured and lying in a hospital somewhere. Don't give up hope.'

Sean checks his phone. 'No news.'

Decima howls louder. 'I told you, he's gone. I can feel it in my heart. Why did he have to be there when it happened.' She sobs hysterically.

My mother hands her a glass of orange juice.

'Drink this, dear.'

Decima swallows it and two minutes later she's fallen forwards onto the table, fast asleep.

'That'll work for a couple of hours,' says Astrid.

'Mrs. Archer, I'm so grateful you are letting me stay. I'll have to go soon and look for work, but I'd really like to be here with Alice for a while longer until we know she's safe. I'll pay you as soon as I get some money.'

'Don't be silly, you're part of the family and we're delighted to have you. Now you can give me a hand to water the plants.'

Off they go together. Sean looks back over his shoulder and I give him a wave and smile. I'm so lucky to have him. He's a good man and I know he'll be a wonderful husband.

Decima is snoring away so I go upstairs to clean and tidy 'our' room. Her clothes are all over the place and there's a heap of wet towels on the floor. I start picking them up, and then I think I can't really be bothered, so I invoke the *Muckless* spell and watch as everything folds or hangs itself up. The bed makes itself and the curtains draw back as the window opens to let the smells from the garden in. The towels gather themselves up and throw themselves out of the door, where Decima has suddenly appeared. They hit her square on in the face.

She pulls them away from her face, and stares at me with her mouth hanging open.

'What am I seeing?' she says.

I take the towels from her, and she slumps down on the bed.

'Would you please tell me what's going on? What happened, how did I get here, and what did you just do? I think I'm hallucinating.'

7

Planning the future

Alice

It's time for me to move back home. As I'm getting ready to leave, everybody fusses around Decima. I give Sean a hug and thank him for staying to help my mother.

'I need to sort a few things out at home, but I'll give you a call tomorrow,' I tell him. He pulls me into the hall, leans me against the wall and puts a finger to my lips.

'Shh,' he whispers.

He strokes my hair, nuzzles my neck, takes my hand and places it on his chest.

'Can you feel that? That's my heart beating out its love for you.'

I leave my hand there, feeling his heart pound as if it's trying to burst out. I rest my head against his shoulder. We stand there silently, rocking slowly until I give a small sigh. 'I need to go now.'

'Let's get married very soon, Alice. Please. I can't wait. Every moment spent away from you is torture.'

I hold his face in my hands and kiss him.

'As soon as everything has settled down, we'll start planning our wedding. I want it as much as you do.'

His face lights up. 'I'll be thinking of you every minute of every hour until I see you again, Alice.'

'So will I, Sean.'

I almost reveal that I've sent his music to Scorpio, but decide to keep that as a surprise for another time.

When I open the door into the kitchen, Zylch has shed the blue neon poodle effect and is back to his sleek silvery beauty. I crook my finger at him and he flies up onto my shoulder and folds his wings, (or are they arms, I can never really work it out) around my neck.

I wave my fingers at Astrid, who nods back and smiles as she massages and brushes Decima's spikey hair.

Cory drives me home, his car weighed down with packets, jars and boxes of food my mother mysteriously produced just minutes before we were ready to go.

'To keep you going for a while,' she said.

As we drive away, Cory says it looks more than enough to keep a small town going for a month.

He asks if I'd thought about what I was going to do now the Tower has gone. We talk about possible insurance payouts and how we all need to find work pretty quickly. It will be easy for him, with all his talents, but I really don't know where to start. I don't have any qualifications and no particular skills.

When we reach my place, we unpack some of the food, grab some beers and settle in the garden with Zylch playing at our feet.

'You know, Sean kind of said you were a witch long ago and I thought he was off his head because he's so infatuated with you. He told me something crazy about you being able to fly him into the sky. Was that really true?'

'Yes. I can do that.'

'For anybody?'

'Yes.'

'For me?' he asks hesitantly.

'Where do you want to go, Cory?'

His whole story comes out. He explains about his twin brother, the title, the castle in England, and why he needs to get there urgently.

I'm not surprised. Even though I'd never met a real aristocrat, anybody could sense that Cory wasn't just an 'ordinary' person. He has an air about him, just the way he talks and carries himself, his manner, tells you he is a gentleman.

Now I realize why he always seemed to be withdrawn, as if in his head he is far away. The bond between twins is unbreakable, so being wronged by his brother must be a very painful wound.

'When do you want to go?'

'As soon as possible. It sounds as if there's not much time left. If I go by plane, it could well be too late. I must get there before Jonty dies.'

'We'll go now, straight away.'

'The dogs…'

'This will have to be a very quick trip, Cory. So quick, you'll be back to see to them.

'Alice, I really appreciate you doing this for me. If I can just be there before he dies and find out what's going on, then I can arrange to go back later. You're an angel and Sean is a very lucky man. I know you will be happy together.' He pauses for breath. Looks at his fingernails. Glances up at the sky, back to me. 'Er, how does it actually work? I mean the flying? What do I have to do? We'll need some other clothes, it's always wet and cold where we're going.'

'Tell you what. We'll drive to Decima's so you can feed the dogs, then we'll pass your place to pick up whatever you need. You don't need to worry about anything else, I'll take care of it all.' I stand up and make to go. 'Zylch, you be good. I won't be gone long. Can you look after yourself until I'm back?'

Zylch does a tap dance and ends up bowing to me.

'I can't get over that creature,' Cory laughs. 'It's so lifelike.'

We drive over to Decima's. When Cory opens the door two scruffy dogs gallop up to him, wagging their tails and licking him all over.

'Hello you two,' he croons, 'I'm going away for a while, but I'll be back very soon. You behave yourselves.'

I knew Decima had two dogs, but I'd imagined them to be sleek and elegant, like her. These two, however, are

stumpy and hairy and both have a distinctly 'doggy' smell.
How interesting. They are not the fashion accessories I
had expected. She must really love them.

While Cory fills their food and water bowls, I prepare
a couple of glasses of juice, adding a single drop of **Dorm**
to his glass. We take the dogs to the beach for a quick
run, then sit sipping our drinks while they settle in their
beds. When Cory's head starts to nod, I take his hand.

'All aboard the Skylark,' I whisper.

'Mmm,' he murmurs.

I summon **Brmstick**, and we land gently in Cory's
courtyard among some potted palms. He opens his eyes
and blinks.

'Did that just actually happen?' he laughs. 'Or am I
losing it?'

His house is immaculately tidy and quite minimalist,
in shades of gray, with large photographic prints on the
living room wall, all seascapes in black and white with one
selective color in each. It feels very zen.

The French doors look out over the sea, glinting silver
in the sunlight.

'Where are we going, Cory? What's the address?'

'The hospital is ten miles from the castle, in the south
of England. Lewes, Sussex.

My knowledge of the geography of England is non-
existent. 'Can we get a 'What3Words' fix on your phone?
That will pinpoint the location.'

'Seems like *aqua.mince.floppy.*' He shows me the map.

OK, grab what you need and we'll be on our way.'

He goes off to find some warm clothes while I brew up a jug of coffee.

He returns with an armful of thick, musty knitted sweaters that look as if they've seen better days.

'Help yourself. Sorry, best I can do. They've been in storage since I left England. Don't really know why I kept them, but just as well because we're going to need them. Heaven knows what people will think when they see us.'

I pick a thick, creamy-colored knit with a complicated twisted pattern and pull it over my head. It's heavy and scratchy on my neck.

'Aran,' Cory says. 'Good choice, it'll keep you warm.'

I hope so, it's not at all comfortable.

'You don't need to worry about how we look.'

'How do you mean?'

'Trust me.'

Without my phone, it's going to be hard work to summon both the **Brmstick** and **Inviz** spells for travel so far.

I hand Cory a mug of steaming coffee, dosed with a heavy shot of **Dorm**. 'Drink this, it will keep you warm.'

I sip my drink and watch him start to relax, until eventually he leans back and closes his eyes. When his chest rises and falls slowly and he lets out a small snore, I know he's ready. I lock fingers with him and summon all my strength and power.

England, here we come.

8

Goodbye old chap

Cory

I close my eyes as instructed. And that's all there is to it. There are no flying sensations, no soaring through the clouds to symphonic music as Sean had described.

Boom, and here we are. Side-by-side on an orange bench in a cold NHS hospital Accident and Emergency waiting room. It's full. Everybody sits patiently in rows, some in clear distress. Nobody takes a blind bit of notice of us. Alice takes my hand and we slip out into the maze of identical brightly-lit corridors.

When I notice that we are still being royally ignored wherever we go, Alice tells me that she'd purchased the In-App invisibility add-on so that we wouldn't be hindered. We must keep touching, she warns me, and must not speak, because although we can't be seen, we can still be heard. Phew! I thought Alice had suddenly developed a newfound crush on me. Although I'm very fond of her, my infatuation with her all that time ago is long gone. I'm relieved there's no disloyalty to Sean.

No less than three nurses are at my brother's bedside,

measuring his pulse, staring at the heart monitor, shaking their heads at each other and pursing their lips. They look very concerned. Traumatized, really. For there is somebody else at the bedside, too, yelling orders at the top of her voice.

'I don't give a fig what them rules are. Do it NOW, we haven't got all day.'

Arrogant, rude, entitled – here before me is the female version of Jonty made flesh.

'No we don't, Erica… Can't you see that isn't possible? He's never going to sit up again.'

'WHAT did you just say? Don't you DARE use my first name. Who do you think you are? It's Lady Cholmonderly if you please.' She paused here, to take in her own voice. My heart leapt into my throat. What??

Her small thin mouth puckers slightly into a smirk. 'Or it will be very soon, you can be the first. You cheeky little madam. Now get him sitting up. The vicar will be here any minute.'

'Chumley, you ignoramus,' I call.

Alice hisses and digs her elbow into my side.

'OI!' I yell.

Erica looks over her shoulder.

'CholLMONderly indeed!' I mutter. Never have I felt such violence rise within me.

Confused, Erica follows the direction of the medics' eyes and turns towards us. As she does so, a glint of silver, red and gold flashes beneath the glare of the overhead lights. I glance at Alice to see if she has seen what I've just seen. Alice isn't visible of course, and I find myself staring at the legs of a TV monitor.

I turn back to examine this creature again. Yes, there it is again. I'm not seeing things. Balanced precariously on top of a ponytail rising like a fountain from the crown of her head, in a style I believe is known as the Croydon Facelift, something is catching the light. Is that a tiara I can see?

My heart thunders, blood rushes to my face, my ears are red hot. I'm sweating all over. The only person more furious than this woman now is me. All the work I've done on myself over the years, all the masterclasses, meditations, breathing techniques, sound baths, quantum jumping, cold water therapies, all of them dissolve back into the most possessive mist of anger I've ever felt in my life. I wouldn't be surprised if there are two visible streams of steam funneling out of my ears.

I know exactly what I have to do. I let go of Alice's grip and surge forwards.

'No!' Alice screams.

Erica jumps and then freezes, mid-shriek, to the spot. The nurses stare at me, six pairs of eyes pinned white-wide, jaws on the floor.

'I know what you are up to,' I pinch Erica's throat and snarl into her face. I nearly pass out from the whiffs of bad breath, alcohol and perfume.

I feel the weight of Alice on my back, wrestling me to

the floor. She wraps her arms around me and drags me away from the bed and back into invisibility.

Not knowing what has hit her, Erica whimpers like a wounded dog and darts her eyes around, fiddling with her ponytail. The medics, frozen to the spot, look like they've just seen a ghost. Which, in a way, they have. Only Jonty, lying there, close to death, looks calm and peaceful. More serene than I've ever seen him. My throat thickens. So this is it. Death, it seems, would suit my idiotic twin bro.

'I've seen enough,' I gasp, grabbing hold of Alice's arm.

I dodge my way through the perplexed group towards the bed, taking Alice with me this time, and touch Jonty's hand.

'Goodbye old chap.' Blinking back the tears, I turn to take one last look at Erica.

9

Letting go

Alice

I drop a dozy Cory back at Decima's and ***Brmstick*** home. At the end of the lane, I dismount and walk the last few yards. I've just clicked the gate shut when my neighbor calls out: 'There's been a young guy here looking for you. He's got an eye patch? Are you OK?'

'I'm fine, thanks. Just a bit tired.'

'Give me a shout if you need anything.' He waves his hand and closes his door. When I walk indoors I feel a great sense of relief. I'm home, and tonight I'll sleep in my own bed. How many days has it been since the Tower burned? It feels like so very long ago.

My mind goes back to those few minutes spent with Sean. I'd surprised myself by my response. Had I had finally accepted Sean's love?

Exhaustion hits me like a truck. Mentally and physically I am empty. I slump down on the edge of my bed and close my eyes. I'm vaguely aware of gentle hands pushing my head down to the pillow and lifting my legs onto the bed, then wrapping a cover over me. A soft hand strokes my hair, and a small silky head snuggles into my neck.

Next morning, I'm woken by a spear of sunlight hitting me between the eyes. I slowly stretch my arms wide, enjoying the smell of coffee and the glorious space of my own bed after a good night's sleep. I swing my legs over and sit up. Beside me is a mug of brown liquid and a large piece of Parmesan cheese with specks of mold on the rind.

'Blekfast,' says Zylch proudly.

I stroke his head while he watches as I politely drink the hot water and coffee grounds and nibble around the mold on the cheese.

'Thank you, Zylch. That was very thoughtful of you.'

'Taking - care - of - Alice,' he chants. With a little bow he hops up onto the windowsill.

In the bathroom I swill my mouth with water to dislodge the crumbs and coffee grounds left from my 'blekfast.' A haggard face with baggy eyes, dull skin, lank hair and dry cracked lips stares back from the mirror. I can't remember the last time I had a proper shower or washed my hair. Decima showering twice a day took all the hot water so there was none left for me.

I stand beneath the powerful jet of hot water until it runs cold, leaving my skin tingling, then I wrap myself in my toweling dressing gown and sit outside, listening to the bird song and the drone of farm machinery in the far distance, soaking up the warmth of the morning sun. Zylch has transformed himself into a penguin and is swimming around in the pond, looking to check that I'm watching him.

What now? How will I find a new job, without any qualifications? What's going to happen to Decima? How long can she stay with my parents? Josh is dead – shouldn't we be organizing some kind of memorial service for him? Cory is fighting for his inheritance. Ramon has gone. Who or what was responsible for the fire at The Tower? Why is a man with an eye patch looking for me? Everything seems so upside down. It's all tumbling around in my head, then I suddenly remember I promised to call Sean today. If he doesn't hear from me soon, he'll panic and come here, and as much as I love him, I really do want some time to myself for a little while, so I'll have to replace my phone which was destroyed in the fire.

With no energy to **Brmstick**, I stroll down the path through the field and catch the next bus into downtown Hawk Bay City. The skyline has changed dramatically now The Tower is no longer there dominating the town. When the bus drives slowly past the fenced off site I can't help but think of all the times I spent there, the good and the bad, and feel a wave of sadness.

It's going to take four hours for the shop to set up a new phone with my old number, so I decide to wander around town. First, I go down to the harbor and sit for a while looking out to sea. I remember that day when the old lady was mugged, and Jai first spoke to me, and I fell in love. I shake my head, because that is all in the past. Recalling that time when I walked with kind, caring Josh, tears sting my eyes knowing I'll never see him again. I walk back through the rough end of town, passing the little flower shop called 'Flowers R'Us', where I used to stop and chat with the old lady owner. Today there are no buckets of flowers ranged on the pavement, no flowers in the shop. When I push the door open the glass windchimes tinkle.

'We're closed,' says a voice from the back room, hearing my footsteps.

'Hello,' I call. 'It's Alice.'

I find the old lady sweeping down some shelves surrounded by empty pots and boxes.

'Ah Alice. How lovely of you to come by. I was worried after that terrible fire. What an awful shock. All those poor people. Are you alright?'

She turns her wrinkled face to me, her faded blue eyes crinkled up in a smile.

'I'm fine, Mrs Blossom. What are you up to? No flowers today?'

'No dear. I'm clearing up. Closing down. It's long past time for me to retire, and I can't compete with the flower shops in the town center. As soon as I've sold, I'll be moving to Florida to live with my son and his family.'

'I'll miss you,' I say, 'you've been here for as long as I

can remember.'

'Thirty-five years. Can you imagine! I don't know where the time has gone,'she chuckles.

I notice how her back is bent and her hands are swollen. She can't reach the higher shelves.

'It won't be the same here without you. But I'm happy to think of you enjoying the Florida sunshine, surrounded by your family.'

'Would you like a cool drink?' she asks. 'I could do with a little break.'

While she shuffles away I flick a **Muckless** spell at the shelves and around the room so that by the time she returns it's all clean and tidy.

'Here you are.' She pulls out an old bench so we can sit side by side and drink lemonade. Glancing around at the neatly stacked pots and boxes, she shakes her head.

'Well, I must be getting forgetful, I didn't realize I'd finished clearing up. So what are your plans, now that The Tower has gone?'

'I don't know, I haven't really thought about it yet. I expect something will come up.'

'Wherever you go, they'll be lucky to have you,' she squeezes my hand.

'You take care, Mrs Blossom. If I don't see you again I wish you the very best of luck.'

'And to you Alice. Thank you for stopping by. I'm so pleased to have seen you. I'll be locking up for good once I've finished cleaning in here. Just wait a moment and let me see if I can find something for you before you go.'

She searches through some drawers beneath the shop counter, then gives a sigh. 'Nothing left I'm afraid. Not even a dried flower. I am sorry, I'd have liked to leave you something to remember me by.'

I walk to the door, turning to smile at her. 'I'll always remember you, Mrs Blossom. Be happy.'

The windchimes tinkle with a final wave as I leave.

I've gone about fifty yards when I hear panting, and a voice gasping '*Alice! Alice!*'

Mrs Blossom is hobbling after me, waving a packet in her hand.

'Here! Keep this, and may it bring you luck!'

She tucks it into the pocket of my jacket, and totters away.

I walk to where the Tower had stood, and peer through a gap in the fence. There's a tangle of metal, a heap of glass shards, singed papers, broken pieces of office furniture. A voice behind me tells me to move on, and a security guard ushers me away. I explain that I used to work there and ask if he knows when the site will be cleared. He shrugs, saying the police and insurance company are conducting forensic investigations and nothing can be touched until they've finished. As I turn away he pats me on the shoulder.

'Good luck, honey. I hope you find a new job soon.'

Threading my way through the streets, my feet lead as if of their own volition towards my old apartment. I stop and look up at the window. A woman's face briefly stares back at me and then turns away. I look at the doorway where Jai used to wait for me. Everything reminds me of him today.

I walk slowly to Mumtaz, the restaurant where we used to meet. Each time the door opens those familiar aromas waft in the air, and I inhale them deep into my lungs. As they fade away, I know it's time to finally let go of Jai.

On impulse I buy a small wooden boat from a nearby toy shop and take it back to the harbor. I write 'Goodbye Jai' on the cotton sail, and drop the boat over the harbor wall, into the sea. It spins around slowly in the current and then starts to bob away. I watch it until it disappears out of sight.

The instant I collect my new phone and switch it on it's flooded with missed calls, and messages. All from Sean.

I call him straight away.

'I've been in bits! Where have you been? I've been calling for hours. I was just about to come to find you, I was so afraid you were hurt.'

How very lucky am I to have somebody who loves me so much?

'Remember I lost my phone in the fire? I've been to town to get a new one. You didn't need to worry, but it's so sweet that you did. You are so lovely Sean.'

'I'll always worry unless I have you in sight. You are

so precious to me, Alice.'

'How is everything there? How's Decima?'

'It's fine. I think she's loving all the fuss she's getting. And guess what? Your mother is going to teach me how to make some kind of special skin cream. Apparently, it's a formula that only she knows, and she will trust me with it. That makes me feel so proud.'

I gulp. 'Well, that's great. It will keep you from getting bored, and it shows just how much you are a part of the family now.'

'When can I come to see you?'

'I'm really looking forward to seeing you, but I'm so tired and I need a couple of days to just relax on my own. Would you mind very much?'

I hear the disappointment as he hesitates.

'Not at all. I'm missing you like mad, but I want you to rest as much as you need. Just keep in touch on the phone, will you?'

'I promise. And if I do need any help, I'll let you know straight away.'

'I love you so much Alice.'

'I love you too, Sean, and I'll see you very soon.'

'That's the first time you've said that,' he whispers.

'Then I'll say it again. I love you Sean.'

I click off the phone and walk to the bus stop with a lighter, bouncier, step. I'm making a new start. Where it will lead, I don't know, but I feel a sense of peace.

Zylch is waiting for me and jumps up into my arms.

He peers into my eyes, and says: 'Alice is harpy?'

I laugh and kiss the tip of his nose. 'I think you mean happy, Zylch. I certainly hope so! And you're right. I'm truly happy. Everything is going to be fine.'

10

What's in the basement?

Decima

I pace up and down the cluttered kitchen, picking up and dropping random bits of junk as I go.

'You lied to me, Cory.'

'There were no lies, Decima.'

'I thought we were close?'

'I was a basketball pro. And after my accident I became a butler. Naked butler sometimes, yes, that's true too, until I came to CGO TV and joined your team. I didn't mention the title that's all. It's a nonsense. Meaningless. My brother had taken on that role in any case. So, technically…'

'Legally?'

'He is the eldest, by three minutes, so, yes.'

One of his long, black denim-clad legs sticks out sideways from the bench. I kick his foot.

'Please, Decima, I'd rather not talk about it right now. There's something I want to ask you. Well, not a question, more of a, a propo, a propos…'

I freeze in my tracks. A proposal?

'…a proposition.'

I resume my pacing. I'm an idiot. Who'd propose to me?

It's impossible to get angry at Cory for long. He won't have it. He'll clam up until you find yourself melting into those oh so truthful brown eyes of his. That's why his lie – OK deception, withholding of the truth, whatever you want to call it – is such a shock.

'What next? Oh – and I'm dead. Have you ever been dead, Cory?' I grab the rammed to overflowing cutlery basket and shake it upside down on the draining board. Metal clashes against metal. 'You lose everything.'

I scoop up a handful of forks and smash them down on the floor. 'I've lost my looks, my work, my home, my dogs…' I return to the table, snatch a jar of paste, bang it on the table. Next to it is a black book covered in candlewax, I pick it up and raise my arm.

Before I can throw it, Cory leaps forward and snatches it away. 'Stop this now!'

A single, horrible, high-pitched, screech erupts from below.

We freeze and lock eyes.

'What was *that*?'

'There's something very sinister going on in their basement, you must have noticed,' Cory says.

'Witchy things. I'm getting used to it.'

He goes to the sink and fills a kettle, 'They only have instant coffee here.'

'Touché. I've adapted.'

'Sit!'

I obey.

'Now breathe.'

I do the slow, outward breath exercise he taught me. 'So everybody can have their pets, even killer pets, close to them except me.'

'I know it's tough for you.'

How are they?'

'They're doing well,' he says carefully.

'They are my life, Cory.'

'I know that. Why do you think I've moved into your place? I mean, it's a very *nice* place too. But it's all about Twinkle and Barney, and I get it. They're getting lots of cuddles, lots of treats. They miss you.'

'You're very kind. I'm sorry I shouted.'

'Barney sits by the door every night waiting for you to come home.'

'Does he really?' I pick at the drips of one of the fat cream candles lined up on the table.

'Why can't I have them here, Cory? Why?'

'You're in hiding,' he says quietly.

'But we're in the middle of nowhere.'

'They could give you away, I guess. And there could be other reasons.'

'I suppose so.' I think about Astrid's furtive

movements in the garden, hauling large, heavy trash bags towards Sean's shed. '

Cory makes the coffee and we sip in thoughtful silence.

'You do have to lie low, Decima.'

'Lie low living a lie.' I pick a grape from the bowl. 'While all this time you've been the one living a lie. 'Who else knew about this? Alice I suppose?'

'Only recently. She's been very helpful.'

'Astrid?' I nod towards the garden. 'Where's she gone? She was there a moment ago. How has it come to this?'

Cory pushes his hair back. 'Look. I've got a problem. There's been another death, unfortunately. Er. My brother.'

'What? Cory! Why didn't you say?'

'I did start to explain, and then you got shirty. But truly, nothing to be sorry about. We weren't close. Josh going has upset me far more.'

'Josh… oh Josh. It's unbelievable isn't it.'

Cory moves behind me and wraps his arms around me. 'The thing is,' he says softly into my ear, 'I do have to return to the UK to sort out a very sticky problem. Probate, wills, inheritance and all that.'

The stable door clatters open and Astrid bundles in from the garden with yet another trash bag. 'What's going on? Oh dear, oh dear, what now?' She puts her arms around both of us.

'Such times, such difficult times.'

'Take that away from me, it stinks!' I squeal.

'Sorry,' she backs off and makes for the sink. 'More coffee?'

Behind my back, I sense an exchange of looks between Cory and Astrid.. I spin round.

'What's going on?'

11

House sitting

Cory

Small spaces make more sense to me. How many sofas can you sit on at once? How many beds can you sleep in, bathrooms shower in? But I'm beginning to see what living in an expensive piece of real estate is all about. There are these cool mullioned windows on the ocean-side with French doors leading onto a broad brick terrace. Perfect for stretches at dawn to whisky on the rocks at sundown. The combination of the low overhanging trees, twisted by the elements, and great tubs of grasses and bamboo rustling in the wind soothes the soul. Kind of a contained wildness is what it is, I guess, with all the comforts of home to hand.

You can only see the sea if you lean over the sheer drop, but you can always hear it. And feel it throughout the house come to that. There's an invisible mist, no matter what the weather. The presence of the ocean usually calms me, but today I'm feeling antsy.

I fix a large sundowner and take it to the terrace. I don't sit down but pace, rattling the ice in my glass, listening to the waves, searching for the inner peace that has deserted me. Staying here without her being here is disturbing. That's the truth of it.

Why can't I be comfortably alone anymore? Is it something to do with Josh and Jonty going so suddenly. Am I really falling for her? Having a crush, falling in lust, falling *in love*, whatever, is simply your mind telling stories to itself. Your own brain projecting all sorts of crazy onto the person of your fixation. But where does the brain meet the body, exactly? It's bodily, this yearning to physically possess. But we already have that! That's the crazy part. We've been lovers for years now. We each know our place in the scheme of things. Sex is a functional need for Decima and for us guys. We thought we'd solved that so neatly, sharing Decima between us without envy or possessiveness. What has changed? Well, there's only three of us four guys left now. And, with one of us loved up with Alice, and the other living it up in South Korea, that brings it down to two. One on one.

Maybe it's simply missing the physical? I'm sleeping in her bed so I'm bound to notice she's not there. But no. Something chemical is going on. Infatuation? Like when we all had a crush on Alice? Sean really was in love. And is. They're happy together. We're all happy for them too. These thoughts spin on and on, backwards and forwards in time.

I go inside to pour myself another drink, but stop in time. Instead, I give in to the two pairs of brown eyes gazing longingly at me and take the dogs for a run. With a nod to the security guard, I set off along the cliff top and let the wind blow me senseless.

Decima's place is on the doorstep of some of the wildest beaches around. Too far out of town for the druggies and muggers. But with 24-hour security and still well inside the Deliveroo zone. It's about as private and safe as you can get in a crime-ridden city like Hawk Bay. That's what rich gets you.

Returning from our walk, I get a cozy sense of coming home. So much comfort. But always, always the same question. Why isn't she here? How will this ever be resolved? This is her place. She should be here.

I throw the keys in the Chinese bowl in the small circular hallway and push open the carved oak door that leads to the living room. The dogs race across to their water bowls by the breakfast bar. Apart from the open-plan kitchen, it's all weirdly old-fashioned for such a modern house, with parquet floors, old rugs, oak bookcases stashed with books lining the walls and huge, deep cream sofas. The centerpiece is a large mantle with an open fire. Decima's favorite spot.

It's cold but I leave the fire unlit, sink into the sofa and check my phone.

Ramon is online.

I message. He calls.

'Hey!'

'Hey yourself.'

'Where are you?'

'I'm at Decima's, looking after the pooches. I'm sorry I can't really talk too much about what's going on here, man.'

'You think Gauld's listening in?'

I grunt noncommittally.

'I get it. Them slimy tentacles leech everywhere, man. They're probably around here somewhere too. You can't be too careful. How are you doing? You OK, Cory?'

I swallow hard. That can be the worst question sometimes. 'I got a lot on.'

'So sorry man. I heard about your brother too. That's tough.'

'I'll be flying to the UK any day now. My brother was a wastrel, Ramon, it was only a matter of time. Josh has affected me more. It's hard to believe. Has it sunk in with you yet?'

'To be honest, I'm burying it right now. I'm so busy, and I'm in such an alien place, nothing makes sense anymore. I'm hitching a ride to wherever it takes me, babbling in a language I can't understand... Stand here. Go over there. Look this way. Look that way. Open your eyes. Close your eyes. Cry. *Acting*, man, it's harder than you think.'

'Is that producer woman around. What was her name?'

'Michiko Kim. Yeah she's hovering. Around *me* most of the time. Showing me off at all these parties and brand events. Then I got this minder, translator, spy guy, but I have to suck it up.'

'It's your big break.'

'It's what I wanted. We're going to some fancy dinner tonight at a kisaeng house. You heard of that? It's like the geisha in Japan. They live on this freaking hill right in the center of Seoul. It's crazy man.'

'You're getting a geisha?'

'I don't know about that. It's like thousands of bucks a go just for a cup of tea. I don't need no geisha, the women here are so hot. All you have to do is go get a haircut. You heard of a Korean haircut?'

I smile and snuggle down onto the sofa some more. 'Is it what I think it is?'

'Man!.'

'Out in the open?'

'Well no. There's back rooms.'

I don't react but keep my voice at a positive high. 'If that's your average barbershop what's the geisha house going to be like?'

'Kisaeng. That's it, man. I have no idea. I'll let you know. Hey, I wish you were here with me. We'd have some fun times.'

I press my lips tight together. I can't think of anything worse than a seedy back-room experience with some poor girl trying to make a living any way she can. I think I'm ready to settle down. I think that's what's going on with me right now.

12

Snake milker

Alice

When I wake next morning, I find Zylch in the yard sunbathing. There's a mug sitting on the table. Oh dear, I think he's made coffee again.

He jumps into my arms and hugs me. 'I love you Alice,' he giggles. 'Made you a nice drink.'

'How kind you are,' I say, picking up the cold mug. Oh my goodness, surely not cold coffee.

Zylch is watching me as I take a sip.

'Good?' he asks. 'Better than coffee?'

'Good? It's sensational, delicious. I've never tasted anything like it! How did you make it?'

'Frowers petals. Lots of frowers, and things.'

'Flowers and things? What sort of things?'

'Just things,' he chirps.

'How did you know how to make it?'

'Secret,' he giggles, skipping away and doing a series of backward flips.

Even this early in the morning, the sun is already hot,

and I lean back and close my eyes. Where do I go now? I need to find a job, but where to start without any educational qualifications?

I pick up my phone and flick through the job vacancies in Hawk Bay City, drawing up a list of opportunities.

Shipping clerk, training given. Receptionist. Room attendant. Waitress. Fundraiser. Telesales. Pet food taster. Snake milker. Candy maker. Hm, maybe. Personal shopper. Mermaid! Professional Mourner. Museum tour guide.

I cross off the first six immediately because I can't imagine sitting in an office all day, followed by the pet food taster which is not for vegetarians. Snake milker could be interesting. Candy maker I could do but would probably eat all the candy. Personal shopper? I think you need fashion sense, which rules me out. Mermaid — now that sounds tempting, as long as the water's warm. Professional mourner? When I think about it, it's very sad and I don't think I'd feel comfortable getting paid to mourn for somebody I didn't know, but then if it makes the family feel better to have more mourners, I suppose it's a possibility. Museum guide, that could be another interesting one.

I make a shortlist: Snake milker. Mermaid. Museum guide.

Snake milking intrigues me the most, I think I'd enjoy it and love the idea that my skills would save lives. Sadly, when I check out the qualifications and licenses required, my hopes are dashed, although there is one possibility where it says trainees are welcome to apply. Enthusiasm and quick learning more important than experience.

Mermaid sounds fun, and you don't need any training. You wear a mermaid costume and swim to entertain people at parties. I read through everything required, yes, yes, yes, yes, I can do all those. Then no. I cannot swim underwater, because I can't hold my breath for long and I panic. What a shame, I know that could be such fun otherwise.

That leaves museum guide. There are only two museums in Hawk Bay City, one features clowns and garden gnomes, two of my phobias, and the other is a collection of medical instruments dating back thousands of years and requires extensive knowledge of archeology, metallurgy, anatomy and petrology, whatever that is, and which I definitely don't have.

So for the moment that leaves snake milking, which carries a pretty good salary. I pick up the phone and call. I'm thrilled to be invited for an interview this afternoon, although the man on the phone does warn me they have a long list of applicants. He tells me to bring my driving license. Luckily I have one, although I don't own a car. I've never really needed one, but my father insisted because 'You never know when it might be useful'.

The HBC Snake Venom Extraction Facility has a small office downtown, on the first floor over a tattoo artist. I'm feeling a mixture of nerves and excitement. There are four other candidates ahead of me. They look kind of rough, a group of three who are all together, and another one who can't be more than twelve. I feel ridiculously out of place and certainly unlikely to get the job.

The young kid comes out in two minutes, scowling and slamming the door. 'Course I can drive a goddam car.'

The three guys come out laughing and elbowing each other. One of them leers at me and says: 'You're welcome to come and wrangle my snake any time, honey.' The others scream with laughter. I smile back at them sweetly and cast a *Buzz* spell and watch as they frantically swipe at their faces and necks, ducking from an imaginary swarm of wasps only audible to them.

A smartly-dressed man opens the door and ushers me in. There's a logo on his jacket that says: 'HBCSVE', and across the front of his green T-shirt is a picture of a large snake with its mouth gaping open to show long, sharp fangs.

'Hi, thanks for coming in. I'm Steve, HR Manager. So tell me why a pretty lady like yourself would want to get involved with venomous snakes?'

'It sounds interesting, something different. I'm not keen on sitting around in an office all day.'

'And how do you feel about handling reptiles?'

'I'm not at all afraid of snakes. There are plenty where

my parents live, I'm quite used to them. They are beautiful creatures.'

'OK. Now, you say you have a driving license?'

'I do, but at the moment I don't have a car.'

'Well, this is your lucky day, because this job provides transport. Picks you up from town, drives you out to the facility, and brings you home again in the evening. How does that sound?'

'Pretty good!'

'I need to ask if you have any kind of criminal record, or driving offenses. The work we do at the facility is extremely sensitive and top secret. It is part of a government research establishment therefore discretion is vital. Loose tongues can cost lives, many lives. If you are offered the position, you will have to sign an anti-disclosure act, legally binding you to secrecy regarding our work. I should warn you that any breach of this agreement carries a term of imprisonment of at least ten years. Do you understand that?'

'Yes. I will be more than happy to sign if I am lucky enough to be given the job.'

He stands up and holds out his hand.

'Thanks, Alice. I am seriously impressed. You could be perfect for us. I need to consult with our facility coordinator. I'll be in touch.'

There's quite a bounce in my step as I leave the office. I decide to jog home, a sure sign I'm starting to recover from the events of the last few days. Zylch is waiting to greet me and jumps up into my arms.

'I think I've got the job, Zylch! It sounds so exciting – I'm going to be working with snakes!'

'Snakes,' he replies. 'You said snakes aren't cute.'

'Yes, I did say that, because 'cute' means something that is cuddly and you want to hug – like you, and snakes aren't really like that, so some people are afraid of them. I'm not, though. I really want this, Zylch.'

When my phone rings an hour later, I get the news I was waiting for. I have the job, provided I pass the snake handling test tomorrow. I need to be in Hawk Bay City at 8.00 am the next day to be driven to the facility. Mobile phones are not allowed, so I should leave mine at home.

Next morning I'm so excited that I'm waiting at the meeting place at 7.40 am. There are two other women there but they ignore me. A black van arrives, and the driver gets out, wearing a similar T-shirt to the one Steve wore yesterday. He slides open a side door.

'In you go ladies,' he says. I follow the two silent women inside and sit on a cushioned bench. He closes the door, gets into the cab and starts the engine. From where we are sitting, we can't see anything. The back of the van has no windows and a screen between us and the cab prevents any view through the front. I ask the ladies if they've been working at the facility very long, but they stare back at me vacantly as if they can't understand what I'm saying.

The journey takes longer than I had expected. After

twenty minutes I feel the van making a steep descent before coming to a halt. The driver slides open the side door and speaks into a vent in the wall bearing a sign: DANGER OF DEATH. ENTER AT YOUR OWN RISK. He ushers us out into a floodlit tunnel and through a heavy door. I feel a momentary panic, realizing I have no idea where we are. Have I made a terrible mistake? A wave of claustrophobia comes over me so strong, I break out in a sweat. The two women walk briskly through the door, and, with no other choice, I follow them into a small bright room.

A uniformed guard looks us over, waves a metal detector over us and then opens a grilled door and directs us down a corridor.

At the end of the corridor the two women turn to the right and disappear, and I'm left standing wondering where to go next, when a smiling man appears.

'Aha, you must be the lovely Alice, our new snake milker trainee. Steve spoke most highly of you. I'm Ed. Come on in and we'll run quickly through the formalities and then get you started.'

I follow him into a spacious office, the walls lined with files.

'Before we go and meet Big Harry, I'll need you to sign these two pages.'

He pushes the sheets over the desk. One is to say that I understand there may be risks of injury, and I will not hold the organization responsible.

'Don't worry, Alice, we've never had an injury yet. In the extremely unlikely event of a bite, we have all the necessary medical equipment and treatments here to take care of you. It's what we do, after all!' he laughs.

I sign it and the non-disclosure agreement.

'OK, let's go and meet Big Harry and see how you two get on. After that, there's the driving test, and if you pass both – which I am certain you will – you'll be onboard!'

He leads me to a door at the back of his office with a danger warning notice in big red letters.

I'm expecting a vast room filled with shelves of vivariums and am disappointed to find one solitary sleeping snake curled up in a plastic tray.

Ed lifts Big Harry out, and although I don't know very much about snakes, I know a python when I see one.

'Big Harry is a python, isn't he? They're not venomous.'

Ed chuckles. 'Indeed young lady, you're quite right. We use Big Harry here to see how new employees react when handling snakes, and there's no risk involved. Are you ready?'

'Sure. He's not really that big, is he?' If you straightened Big Harry out, I doubt he'd even measure three feet.

'It's all part of the selection process,' says Ed as he drapes Big Harry over my shoulders where he hangs like a wet pillow. 'We want to scare people, see how they react when we tell them his name! But he's only a ball python, he's never going to be a big boy. They don't grow much.'

I put one hand under Big Harry's head and raise it towards my face. He stares into my eyes and his tongue flickers out as he moves on my shoulders to make himself comfortable. I stroke his head, enjoying the feel of his warm body, something between soft leather and silk as his muscles contract his entire length.

'Well, you've passed that test with flying colors. Just the driving to do.'

'Can I see some of the snakes we'll be working with now?'

'Yep, as soon as the driving test is over. That will mean you're a member of the team, and I can show you into the snake pit.' He roars. 'Only joking! Our bad boys are in a different area of the facility. You'll soon be seeing them. Now I'm taking you through to John, who'll get you out on the road.'

He leads the way back into the corridor and down to the far end. There are no windows anywhere; the corridor is illuminated by strip lighting. It feels as if we've walked half a mile before we arrive at an elevator that takes us down to a garage where there are a dozen vehicles parked up. Large trucks, pickups and saloon cars.

'Ho John!' Ed calls, raising his arm and signaling to a man loading cardboard boxes into a pickup.

John ambles over, winks at Ed and nods at me.

'OK Ma'am, please come with me.' He opens the sliding door into a van like the one I came here in and tells me to sit in the back. 'Security rules. Only Level 1 staff know the location of the facility. I'm taking you up to the driving test circuit.'

Again, I'm sitting in a vehicle with no idea where I am or where I'm going, but having met Ed and realized this place is a proper organization, I'm no longer anxious, just intrigued.

Twenty minutes later we arrive. John lets me out into a yard fenced with steel mesh. He unlocks a gate and drives in, pulling up next to a red pickup.

'Your chariot awaits,' he smiles.

It's been a couple of years since I drove, but after driving around the compound for a few minutes I'm confident.

John gets in the passenger seat and I drive out of the compound onto a small lane leading onto a minor road.

'You're doing great. I can see you know how to handle a car. We'll take a little drive to South Basin, I've got a delivery to make there.'

I follow his directions until we reach the outskirts of a small town. 'Now pull up over there,' he indicates a space in front of a hardware store.

'Hey,' he says. 'I need to see someone at the garage. Would you mind taking this package to Marcus in the store?'

I take the package from him and walk into the store looking for Marcus.

A big man with silver hair and a matching mustache

calls out: 'Are you looking for Marcus? You have something for me?'

I hand him the packet, and he gives a bow. 'Thank you little lady. May I ask your name?'

'I'm Alice. I'm going to be working at the snake milking facility, I hope.'

'Well, I am most charmed to make your acquaintance Alice. I guess we'll be seeing each other fairly often.'

On the drive back to the facility, John says he is going to give me a 100% score for my driving. I ask why driving is so important, as the organization provides transport to and from town.

'Well there's a fair amount of driving goes with the job. You can't be milking snakes all day!' He laughs. 'There's plenty of delivery work – anti-venom, equipment, paperwork, a whole load of stuff,' he continues rather vaguely. 'You'll be out on the road most days at least a couple of hours.'

I'm OK with that, it'll be interesting to move around and see new places.

Back again at the facility, John tells Ed I've got top marks for driving. 'No worries about Alice here. Perfect driving. Dropped that package off for Marcus while I was busy. She'll charm all our customers too.'

Ed holds out his hand. 'Congratulations and welcome to the team. Let's get you fitted out, and tomorrow we'll begin your training with the snakes. I'll take you to the canteen so you can get yourself something to eat and drink before we take you home.'

We walk through more long hallways until we reach a large room with vending machines along one wall. 'Help yourself, it's all free, one of our perks to thank our workers.' He gestures at a dozen people standing around drinking and chatting.

'How many people actually work here?' I ask.

'Altogether, couple hundred. But you won't meet many of them. They mostly work in maintenance, keeping the atmosphere running so it's good for the snakes. The technicians keep to the lab, admin have their own area. We work shifts, too. It's a 24-hour job. As a milker, you are in the top echelon. You'll always be day shift too.'

We go to a new area where I'm kitted out with green trousers, leather boots, a green T-shirt emblazoned with the HBCSVE logo, a plain green jacket, a baseball cap with the image of a snake printed onto it and a pair of thick gloves.

'Tomorrow, we'll introduce you to our senior milker who'll start your training.'

'I can't wait!'

He walks me to the heavy metal door I first came through. 'Let's get you home now. See you tomorrow at the same place. And this is by way of thanking you for your work today.'

He hands me two $100 bills.

'But I haven't done anything!'

He winks. 'Sure you have, and there's plenty more where that came from. See you tomorrow.'

I'm driven back to HBC together with five other women who sit in silence. When I try starting a conversation they either stare back at me or close their eyes. Feels like they are told not to communicate.

My head's buzzing when I arrive home. Excitement overload! I can't wait to tell my folks and Sean.

I've only been home a few minutes when I'm surprised to see a car draw up outside my yard. A man steps out and he's wearing a patch over one eye.

'Miss Archer? My name is Rex Tillman and I'm a reporter with the Hawk Bay City Herald. I wonder if there is any chance I could have a few words with you regarding the explosion at the Tower?'

I hesitate.

'I don't think I can tell you anything you don't already know.'

'Maybe not, but I would really appreciate five minutes of your time.'

Zylch has appeared and is winding himself around Tillman's legs.

If Zylch trusts him, that's good enough for me.

'OK,' I say. 'You'd better come in.'

13

A threat and a porcupine

Alice

Tillman sits at the kitchen table while I pour lemonade. Zylch has taken a liking to him and is curled up on his lap.

He asks if I'm able to talk about the fire.

'It must be a terrible shock, losing two colleagues, so please stop me if it's too painful for you.'

'No, it's alright. I've come to terms with it.'

'Lucky for you that you weren't there at the time. I understand that Decima Gauld was working on the top floor, unable to escape. What a terrible death. Any idea why she'd be there at that time of night? Or why the special effects man would have been there?'

I shake my head, because I don't want to have to lie, but I must protect Decima so that nobody knows she's alive. I can't tell him I was there.

'Anything you can tell me would be useful.'

'I'd help if I could, truly, but I honestly don't know what to say. You probably know more than I do.'

He nods slowly. 'You know, there's no way that explosion at the Tower was an accident. There's been something big going on in Hawk Bay City over the last three years. It isn't good, and it all links back to Cliff Gauld. One way or another I'm going to expose him, so if you hear anything that could be of help, I'd be most grateful if you'd contact me.'

He's so right. The rise in drug use has exploded and is getting worse. What was once a pleasant little city is becoming more and more like the Wild West. There have been so many muggings, burglaries and gang fights that people have become really safety-conscious. Gauld has recently opened a company installing alarm systems in commercial and domestic properties. There are no-go areas which people avoid at night. Even though I am confident in my own powers to deal with any threats, I've started carrying pepper spray. You can't be too careful. It's such a shame.

'I'll certainly let you know if I find anything out. I only met Mr Gauld once, when I signed my contract with the TV station. He seemed like a bit of a gangster, to be honest.'

'That's exactly what he is. He is known to have links to the Mafia, and friends in high places here in the city. He's greedy, ruthless and very dangerous. He's also extremely cunning and so far nobody has been able to pin anything directly on him.'

Tillman stands up ready to leave.

'What about you,' he asks. 'Did you find a new job yet?'

'Yes! It's rather exciting. I've just had my interview and been given the position.'

'Great, well done you. Where is it?'

'It's for a snake milk extraction organization. They're going to train me to handle dangerous snakes and collect their venom to make antidotes.'

He frowns.

'Really? Are they in HBC, because I've never heard of them. It must be very new. Strange there's been no announcement about it.'

'An ad online and then an interview in town. After that a second interview at the facility, when I was told I have the position. They seem like very nice people.'

'So they have premises in HBC? May I ask where?'

I tell him I don't know the exact location of my new job but give him the address of the place I met Steve. I explain about the transport to the facility, my test drive and the secrecy agreement.

'You signed it?'

'Yes.'

He nods thoughtfully and leaves.

An hour later, he's back.

'Alice, I need to talk to you.'

'There is no office in HBC. This is the place where you had the first interview.' He shows me a couple of photos on his phone. The premises above the tattoo shop are empty. There's nothing there.

'There is no such organization as the HBC Snake Venom Extraction Facility. Whatever you signed, forget it. It's a scam. I don't know exactly what's going on, but I have a fairly good idea.'

He asks me to tell him everything I can remember. I explain about the transport van, the silent girls, Big Harry, the large facility with no windows, my test drive and delivering a packet to Marcus at the hardware store in South Basin. And as I remember it all I see how gullible and stupid I've been in my enthusiasm to get the job.

'So you say you thought the place was down in a valley?'

'That's how it felt, on the way there and back. As I said, I couldn't see out of the van, but it definitely descended quite steeply for about twenty seconds, and felt as if it went out by the same way.'

'How long were you in the van? Can you recall?'

'I'd say about twenty minutes getting there.'

'Hm. So it was probably twelve miles or so from HBC. There are no valleys for more than a hundred miles from here.'

He sits silently for a couple of minutes and then suddenly jumps and shouts:

'Alice! You're a genius!'

'What have I done?' I laugh.

'You've found the answer to a question I've been asking myself for months! I've been certain there is somewhere close to town producing the drugs that are swamping HBC. Now I know how they've been able to keep it hidden. It's underground! I finally know what I'm looking for, and I'm fairly sure it's out in the backwoods.'

'You mean that place is actually where they're manufacturing drugs? That would explain why the girls in the van were so silent and nervous? They're working there.'

'That's right. They'll be illegals, immigrant workers without papers. Alice, you MUST NOT go back there. These are extremely dangerous people. I believe they could be responsible for the disappearance of at least four young people over the last three years. I'm certain you were recruited not to milk snakes, but to be an unwitting delivery driver for distributing drugs around the state. That's why they were so insistent on seeing how well you could drive. Venom extraction takes a very long time to learn, and it's highly dangerous. Did you see any snakes?'

'Only the one. Big Harry, the python. I had to hold him to show that I'm not afraid of snakes.'

'Handling a python is quite a different proposition to handling venomous snakes.'

'I knew that! I can't believe I've been so stupid. How could I not have seen how wrong it all was? If you hadn't come along…'

'You're not stupid Alice. Honest, decent folk like yourself accept others as they find them. These people are experts in deception and manipulation. If they were to have the slightest hint that you are on to them, they would not hesitate to kill you. That's why you mustn't go back there. Now that you know what they're up to, it would be too easy for you to make a wrong move and arouse their suspicions. You need to phone and tell them you've changed your mind. Let's find a phone number for them.'

However, the number I had for my first interview is no longer in service and there is no recorded number for the facility.

'I'll write a note and give it to the transport driver tomorrow morning.'

'Don't, whatever you do, get in that van. Give him the note and walk away.'

'I will. I promise.'

'In fact, I've had an idea. Tell me where the meeting point is for you. When the van drives away, I can track it with a drone, which will lead to the facility. Boom!'

'That's clever!'

'Not a word to anybody, Alice. If these people get wind that I'm on to them, they'll disappear before they can be caught. Getting them put away is the key to curing the crime epidemic in town. It is also certain that Gauld will try to kill me again. Neither of us will be safe'

'I will not say anything. You have my word.'

'I'll keep in touch, and you do the same and take care.'

We exchange phone numbers before he drives away,

leaving me feeling a mixture of excitement and disappointment. Although my dream of an interesting job has been dashed, it seems I've stumbled into something that could turn out to be a huge story and I can't help but feel a bit of a thrill.

'Well Zylch, it's back to the drawing board. Tomorrow I'll have to look for a new job.'

Zylch nods his head, then he jumps onto my shoulder and puts his arms around my neck, nuzzling into me.

Next morning I go to the meeting place where today there are six silent girls standing around staring at the sidewalk.

I phone Tillman to tell him I'm there waiting for the driver and he confirms that he's ready to launch the drone. When the van pulls up and the girls climb in, I walk up to the driver, who signals me to get in. I hand him a letter to give to Ed and say I won't be coming. He climbs back in and drives off.

A couple of hours later I'm out in the yard, planting herbs, when a car pulls up and a large man gets out and waddles up to my gate, pushing it open and shouting 'Alice Archer?'

'Hello?'

'Why aren't you at work today?'

'What?'

'You signed a contract with the HBC Snake Venom Extraction Facility. You should have been at work at 9.00 o'clock.'

'I sent a letter to say I won't be coming back. I've changed my mind.'

'Well, missy, let me tell you that you cannot simply *change your mind* because you feel like it. That's not the way it works. You've signed a legal document and if you renege, you will be taken to court. So be a good girl and get in the car. I'll drive you there.'

He walks towards me until he's very close.

'If it's because you're afraid of snakes, don't worry. We need drivers too. Come on.'

'No, really, I'm not interested in working there. Please leave.'

'Honey, I'm trying to be nice. I wouldn't want to see that pretty face wrecked. Come here!'

He lunges towards me and tries to grab my arm.

I throw the **Affliction** spell, and he doubles over, clutching his belly. 'I need your lavatory,' he gasps.

'You're not coming into my house.'

'Please,' he whimpers, 'I'm desperate.'

'You should have thought about that before you came out here,' I reply.

'I was fine a moment ago,' he gasps.

'I advise you to get back in your car as quickly as you can, before I call the police,' I say.

He turns and hobbles away taking tiny, mincing steps. A large porcupine runs out in front of him, shaking its quills.

'What the…,' he yells as he trips over the animal and

starts screaming.

He struggles to his feet and half turns towards me. I can see that he is studded with quills from knee to chest.

'Look at me,' he sobs. 'What is going on in this hell-hole?'

'I suggest you get to a doctor pretty quickly to get those things removed. And it's best if you don't come back.'

He wriggles awkwardly into his car, quills scraping in all directions, and reverses at high speed back to the road.

'Zylch, that was pretty wild,' I say. 'You really hurt that man.'

'Bad man,' he says, returning to his glistening silver-haired form. 'Nearry squashed me.'

'Yes, you're right. He is bad, and I don't think he'll be coming back again.'

Zylch collects a few stray quills scattered over the path, and touches one with his small fingers.

'Ouchy!'

'Yes, very ouchy Zylch. It was a clever idea though. How could I have possibly been so naive to be taken in by those people? I was so excited at the idea of the job. Now I have to start all over again. I've got plenty of money in the bank because I hardly ever spend anything. But if I don't want to use it all up, I've got to find work soon, even if it's something I won't like. Not only that, I can't imagine not having anything to do.'

Zylch nods his head wisely as if he completely

understands every word I've said.

I shower to wash away the horror of the man's visit and then take a lump of parmesan from the fridge and share it with Zylch – it's his favorite.

When he's finished eating he bounces away and returns with my jacket.

'Are we going for a walk, Zylch?'

He puts his hand in the jacket pocket and pulls out a small packet wrapped in brown paper. For a moment I'm puzzled, and then I recall Mrs Blossom running after me when I saw her last week. She had dropped something into my pocket that I had completely forgotten about.

I unwrap the paper to reveal the pretty glass windchimes from the flower shop.

They sparkle in the sunshine, and I hang them from a tree branch and listen to them tinkling.

Zylch climbs up the tree and brings them back to me.

'You don't like them there?'

He puts them back into my hand, scampers away and returns with a small bunch of herbs and flowers that he presses into my hand.

'What, Zylch? What are you trying to tell me?'

Zylch sighs noisily.

For a few moments I stare at the little bunch of plants and the windchime, and then I understand.

'Zylch, you're a genius. I pick him up and swing him round, then give him a hug.

I open my phone to check my bank account, and

phone my father.

'Could you lend me $2,000 please? I'm going to start a business.'

14

A lightbulb moment

Alice

Decima and Cory have gone to England, so all is back to normal when I go to see my parents. As it's a glorious spring day, I **Brmstick** to the Brent Flats and then walk the last mile. Zylch skips ahead as I linger over the snowdrops, violets, ferns and wildflowers, truly appreciating for the first the details of their designs, colors and shapes.

Before I reach the house a figure comes running towards me, arms stretched out like wings, hollering and singing. Sean grabs me, swings me around and hugs me so hard he almost cracks my ribs.

'I've died without you,' he sobs. 'You've been gone so long.'

'Four days, you ninny, and you haven't died.' I hug him back and link arms, with Zylch bouncing between us.

'Come and sit,' my mother places a plate of cookies on the table. 'Coffee?' she stirs a spoonful of instant into a mug of boiling water. 'I've been meaning to ask. Is there something wrong with the coffee I make?'

'I don't think so. Why?'

'Well, Decima only ever drinks half of it.'

'Oh, she has this really expensive stuff, made with a coffee machine. I expect she's missing that.'

Sean sits down next to me and puts his arm round my shoulder.

'So tell me about this idea of yours,' says my father.

'I'm going to open a flower shop in the city. I've made an offer to buy Flowers R'Us from Mrs Blossom, who's retiring. She has accepted my offer, and I have enough to pay for the shop and all the fees, but I need a little more so I can fit it out and decorate it the way I want.'

My father nods. 'And what is your strategy? There are dozens of flower shops already in Hawk Bay City, in far better areas. How do you plan to compete with them?'

'I'll be taking over an established flower shop with existing customers, selling my own cut flowers and potted herbs. My overheads will be minimal and my plants will be fresher and better than anything the other shops sell. I won't be paying a middleman because everything will be grown by myself, and Astrid.'

My mother's head jerks up and after giving me a long, hard stare she nods her head slowly. 'Why not?' she says. 'And all our plants will have a special touch, won't they?' she taps the side of her nose.

'Yes. They'll be more vibrant, more fragrant and more

long-lasting than those from anywhere else. I'll be offering flower arrangement contracts to private homes and businesses, guaranteed to stay fresh and bright for two weeks, as well as bridal bouquets and buttonholes.'

'I imagine you'll be wanting to give the shop a whole new look? It's very dated.'

'Not really, I'm keeping the vintage look except for upgrading the lighting and fascia. Unlike the town center shops, mine is going to be somewhere quiet and peaceful, no gimmicks, just affordable, quality plants.'

'Have you thought of a name?'

'Shamrock!' yells Sean.

'No, although it's a good idea, Sean. The shop will be called 'Blossoms'. I've done a rough sketch of how the outside will look.'

I slide my sketch into the middle of the table so everyone can see it.

'So you're using a very soft, pale green for the exterior walls and door, with 'Blossoms' picked out in gold above the door?'

'Yes, with 'Organic cut flowers and potted herbs' below, also in gold. It's to look simple but classy.'

'OK, I like that. You're going to need help though. Have you thought about that?'

'Yep – Shelley is going to help in the shop, preparing arrangements and setting the plants out. I've already spoken to her. Sean will be doing deliveries.'

'Am I?' asks Sean.

'Sure. On your skateboard.'

Sean punches the air. 'Oh yes!'

'Wait a minute,' says my father. 'Have you checked whether skateboards are allowed in town?'

'Fine from 6.00 am to 6.00 pm. No problem,' says Sean.

'We'll only be using organic flowerpots for the herbs, organic wrapping paper and string for the flowers. No plastics anywhere, no chemicals.'

My father stares at me for a long minute.

'So that's it? Your business idea? Let me make sure I understand. You want to buy and revive a downtown flower shop selling plants grown by yourself and your mother. Everything organic. Shelley helping, Sean delivering orders on a skateboard. Is that it? And you want me to lend you $2,000?'

That is the longest sentence I've ever heard my father speak, and the first time we have ever had anything like a conversation.

'Yes. That's it.'

'Whose idea is this?'

'Well, it was Zylch who suggested it, and once I started thinking about it, it all came together.'

I explain about the windchimes Mrs Blossom gave me and how Zylch picked up on them.

'$2,000 won't go far. Where's the rest of the money coming from? Have you taken a loan?'

'It's my own money, all my savings from when I

worked at the Tower. I only need a little extra to set everything up.'

'When are you opening, and have you planned some kind of advertising campaign?'

'It will be about two months before the contract is signed, but Mrs Blossom has already given me the keys and permission to start decorating and organizing. My friend Rex is going to get things going on social media and the press, and we'll try to get the TV news channel down on the day. Mrs Blossom will ...'

'Who's Rex?' asks Sean sharply.

'He's a journalist who...'

'When did you meet him? How?'

I'm not ready to tell anybody about my disastrous snake milker venture.

'He used to run articles on The Tower, and I bumped into him again a couple of days ago. When he asked whether I had a new job I told him about the flower shop. That's when he offered to help. He's a nice man. He's working on a Netflix documentary exposing Cliff Gauld. He visited here when my mother's garden was trashed, and was badly beaten up afterwards by Gauld's men. He lost an eye.'

'How very convenient that he bumped into you,' says Sean cynically.

'Are you jealous?' I laugh.

Sean blushes and scowls.

'Mrs Blossom will be there for the opening, and we'll

be giving a posy or small pot herb to our first fifty customers.'

'Can you have flowers and herbs ready that quickly?' asks my father.

'Don't worry, Patrick. They'll be ready,' Astrid winks at me. 'I'll start planting tomorrow. I'll do flowers, and Alice can do herbs. You'll be surprised at how quickly they'll grow.'

My father grunts, pulls a wry face and nods slowly, knowing quite well that our growing methods will be anything but orthodox.

'I'm a little concerned by how you intend operating. Is it ethical, competing against businesses selling conventionally grown plants?'

'We'll be charging the same price, not undercutting, and we'll be giving our customers enormous pleasure with the quality of our plants. We're well out of the town center, and the market is perfectly large enough to support another flower shop. All I want to do is to make a reasonable living for us all and provide quality products. I don't see anything unethical about it. Commercial producers use chemicals and artificial growing environments to produce their flowers, not to mention the carbon emissions they create with their greenhouses and transportation. The cut flower industry is notoriously harmful to the environment. Our plants will be home-grown, organic and with a near zero-carbon footprint, so we won't be damaging the environment or hurting anybody.'

He looks at me, and smiles, putting his paint-stained hand over mine.

'Alice, I am so proud of you. For your courage to start your own business, and for how you have thought it all through. I think it's an inspired idea, and I know without any doubt that you'll make it a huge success.'

I blink back tears, at this very first time my father has really connected with me.

Astrid burrows in a cupboard and produces a curvy bottle. 'The celebratory floral champagne I've been keeping it for a special occasion. I think this is the right time.' She places four glasses on the table and pops the cork, which sends an eruption of aromatic, colorful bubbles gushing out of the bottle, and returning themselves neatly into it.

We stand and clink our glasses together. 'Here's to Alice, and Blossoms,' says my father. 'We are all going to do everything we can to help with preparing the shop. Sean, you can paint, I'll do the electrics, and we'll see Alice's plans for the shelving and counter. Astrid – you'll be in charge of plant planning, deciding what is best for the season.

Sean comes and stands beside me, tugging me close to him.

'As soon as the shop is up and running, we'll get married. We'll start thinking about that now, yes? Will we go to Ireland? I'd love you to meet my old friends and family.'

I stroke his face. 'Yes, we'll do that. And as soon as we set the date, we'll crack another bottle of this champagne.'

My glass seems to be empty, although I've only taken a sip. I'm wondering what happened, until Patrick roars with laughter and points to Zylch, who is sleeping in the fruit bowl, lying on his back with his legs in the air, snoring loudly.

'You're little friend is sloshed,' he chuckles.

This is truly a day to remember: the first day I felt my father's approval and affection, and the first time I saw him laugh.

15

A visit home

Decima

Astrid is smoothing my face and neck with a very fine layer of Salvheal. We admire my beauty in the mirror.

'It's not me, though.'

'You can be whoever you want to be, Decima. You're not feeling any soreness?'

'You have the lightest touch and you know it.'

Astrid stands back, 'Then we're done,' she says with an exaggerated wave of her arms. 'I do declare you healed.'

'Really?'

There's something familiar about my new look, I can't put my finger on it. I've gone from a skinny-face super-cool brown-eyed sophisticate with long dark hair to a butter-wouldn't-melt rosy-cheeked, blue-eyed strawberry blond. 'I remind myself of someone,' I say, tipping my chin this way and that, side-eying my profile.

'I was going for Jennifer Aniston?' says Astrid. 'A younger Jennifer Aniston, naturally.'

'Hmm, maybe. Nobody would ever guess what I used

to look like would they.'

'All but for…'

'Yes I get it.'

'That nose of yours has got a will of its own that no magic transformation tools could penetrate.'

'I'm glad. I'll keep it. So I can go sit outside now? I can't stay cooped up in here forever.'

'You could still be spotted. We must practice extreme caution. Gauld is still in town and his goons are on full alert.'

I sniff dismissively.

'But… but… I have a surprise for you. Today is the day. Cory is going to drive you over to your place.'

I spin around from the mirror and stare at her, wide-eyed. But she's smiling and nodding.

'You must stay well-hidden.'

It seems odd that I've got clearance to go visit the dogs but can't sit in the garden here, but I don't draw attention to it.

When Cory arrives, I shoot from that cranky old house like a kid out of detention. I pause on the doorstep and smell the freedom. It's exhilarating. The muddy Brent Flats scrub, scattered with weeds, looks like the most beautiful parkland I've ever seen.

Cory has the roof up so that I'm hidden on the back seat. We set off, bumping over the potholes.

This is all very sudden. There's a tension about him today and his nerves are making me anxious. Has something happened to one of the dogs? Both dogs?

His old V Dub is noisy. I feel every vibration. It stinks too. But the smell is of Cory at least – a cool, musky vibe, the kind of uber-expensive perfume you'd imagine an aristocrat to wear, mixed with wet dog. *My* wet dogs. I'm still not quite sure if he's stringing me along with this. What's more real? Alice and Astrid being witches, Josh being dead, Cory being a Lord? ME being dead. Maybe I am dead. Maybe I'm making all of this up?

I can't bear this silence, it's so unusual for us.

'Can you answer me one thing, Cory.' I shout.

'Sure.'

'Why are Alice's family being so kind?'

'They're naturally kind people.'

'But I've been so mean.'

'You gave Alice her break. Her big break on screen. That's not the reason, though. You haven't been all bad, Decima. You're a fantastic pain in the backside sometimes, but you say it how it is. That's an impressive skill.'

'Alienating most folk.'

'And then…' he continues. 'You're not afraid of your own body, you own your desires. You go after what you want. A lot of people look up to you for that. You give them permission. You're unique, you're you.'

'Hmm.' I go quiet. Whoever I am? 'But they're love-bombing me with kindness,' I persist.

'It's how they are. You've been through a lot. You

nearly died. You've been hidden away too long, reading too many trashy novels, that's your problem now…'

'They are not trashy novels.'

'…obsessed with your own obituaries.'

'You would be too, I bet.'

'Ha, there'll never be anything to write about me. To be honest, I'd rather not know what some journalist has to say about me. Nobody knows what somebody else is like, really, deep down. I mean, take Alice, all the clues were there but we didn't put two and two together, did we? None of us did. Remember the way she'd get from the 17th floor of the Tower to the basement in seconds? And what about the way she disappeared from your party, when you were encouraging all four of us to get with her?'

I shiver. 'You see. That's what happens when I try to be kind. I thought she'd really *want* the experience of making love with you guys. After all, there's nothing like it on this planet earth. The five of us…'

'Oh Cory – Josh…'

We turn in to our thoughts.

'And Ramon,' he says after a while. 'Things are going so well for him in Korea.'

Our usually comfortable silence goes weird again. Neither of us are saying it but we're both thinking the same thing. Ramon is in Korea following his dreams. He swears he'll be back but it won't be any time soon, if at all. And Sean… he and Alice are as good as hitched. With everybody's blessing. That's going to be some wedding. That just leaves… us. Neither of us is built for monogamy, that's what makes us such a great couple.

When I hear the engine settle, I know we're on the freeway and I sit up to look out of the tiny back window. It's incredible to be out in the world again. To see the cars speeding by. People going about their daily lives looking bored. But they're not, are they? Who'd have guessed it. Routines aren't boring. Normal life out there is miraculous.

He changes gear.

'We're nearing your place now.'

'Yes, Cory, I know.'

'Best you hide from security, Grant is off shift but you never know.'

I obey, even though I don't look anything like me anymore, I can't afford to let anything go wrong. We're so nearly there. We sail past the security guard. They're used to Cory's coming and going. But what's this? There's a car parked in my courtyard, a filthy white 4 x 4 jeepster, covered in mud. I recognize it at once.

'Cory, what's going on? What's happened?

16

Cory's request

Cory

Decima is out of the car and marching up the steps to her house, bashing at the door and yelling at me to open up, which sets off a cacophony of barking inside.

Whenever she explodes, I stand back and let it happen. Like any firework, there will be a point where the force maxes out and simmers down, but this is dangerous.

I follow on behind. 'So much for discretion. Let's draw attention to ourselves shall we?' I snap.

'What's *she* doing here? Is it Twinkle? What's happened to Barney? What's going on? Is she inside? How come she has a key?'

Full hysteria.

'Let me get to the door, Decima.'

She snatches the keys from me, 'MY door.'

I start to lose it. 'Tell the whole neighborhood you're back why don't you?' I hiss, taking a quick glance at the security gate.

I kick myself for responding. She's screaming at me now.

The guard hasn't looked up from his phone – more disturbing than if he were openly watching us. Is he in the pay of CGO TV, what's left of it? Is he texting Gauld right now? If Astrid hadn't done such a super job on Decima's looks we could be in serious trouble.

To shut her up, I grab her from behind, twist her around and kiss her on the lips. She responds heartily. Strange because kissing isn't our thing, but she presses into me. Now, the only problem is how to stop her.

'The dogs, the dogs,' I whisper. 'Don't tease them.'

'You started it!' she pulls away, giggling, and gets her key in the door.

It's hard to tell who leaps on who with more force. The dogs onto Decima, or she onto them. The anger has transformed into squeals of delight. Tails are wagging, and tongues are licking.

Behind them stands a small dark woman in a baggy gray tracksuit, beaming.

'What are you doing here, Pam?' Decima says, still with her face in the dogs.

'Is it you?' says Pam, looking at her closely, clearly shocked.

Decima looks up.

'Decima it is – you look so different – I am so happy to see you!'

'Some secret,' Decima snarls.

'Don't worry, I'm good at secrets.'

'What's going on? Tell me. Now.'

'Pam is here to help. Look – I'll have to go to the UK very soon and… the dogs.'

This dog-walker friend couldn't be a better person for the job, but Decima doesn't know the half of it yet.

'Now, listen carefully.'

'I get it. You have to go for your brother's funeral…'

The doorbell rings. I jump out of my skin. Decima tears through the lounge, dodges the kitchen bar and disappears into the downstairs bathroom, slamming the door behind her.

Pam calmly gets up, like she's expecting somebody.

I hear the front door open and close again. She returns with a white paper carrier bag, the dogs jumping up at it in excitement. A musky smell of spice hits the back of my throat. My mouth starts watering.

'Sweet potato, squash and cauliflower curry,' she says. 'I thought we'd need it.'

Oh how right she is. I barely remember to eat these days. Decima gets beers from the fridge. We sit around the breakfast bar and tuck in, not bothering with plates or cutlery.

'How long will you be gone?' Decima asks, fixing her eyes on me. Her new, blue eyes. I feel such a passion for her I do a double-take and for a second or two am lost for words.

'I don't know, is the barebones truth of it. It could be

a long time.'

Pam says some sympathetic words. I nod. But my fluster isn't for my brother. I've been struck by a thought, a feeling, a realization.

'How long does a British funeral take?' Decima asks.

'It's going to be nasty,' I can't look at her. I keep my eyes on my plate. Glancing over to Pam occasionally as if it's she who has asked the question. 'This woman, this *Erica*, has got her claws into my brother and it's going to be quite a business sorting her out. These legal fights can take years to untangle.'

'*Years?*' Decima repeats.

I nod at Pam. The seed is sown. I let Decima absorb this.

'As long as it takes, I'm fine with it,' says Pam. 'Twinkle and Barney will be happy with me and Roxy. The dog walkers have seen the news. They think you're dead and gone. They'll totally buy that I've adopted them.'

'I might as well be, Pam.'

'Sorry. That wasn't very delicately put.'

'You won't be apart from them forever. I promise,' I say, even though I'm not at all qualified to say that. 'When Gauld has your life insurance money, he'll clear off out of town and won't be coming back. Things will change. Eventually.'

'Clear orf, will he?' Decima mocks my accent. 'Then what? I can't be dead forever.'

I smile. To my relief, despite her new look, the old Decima is still inside. I have nothing to say to that. I do fear that's exactly what will happen. But I'm sure that, with the help of the witch family's box of tricks, something can be arranged.

'It's tough for you Decima, but I can't tell you how happy I am to see you, my friend,' Pam stands and finishes her beer. 'And the Pink Pacamacs will feel the same once all of this mess has been sorted out.'

'The who?' I say.

'Our dog-walking group. They will be so happy to see you again.'

Decima flicks a tight smile at me which I return with an open grin. Is she *blushing?* That's a first!

'Now, I must be off…' says Pam. 'Oh, I've brought you some books. We miss you at the book club.'

'Can you wait a little longer, Pam,' Decima pleads. 'Let us leave first, will you. I can't bear to see them go. It's easier if I do the walking away.'

'No,' I interrupt. 'You go on ahead, Pam. We've got a few things to sort out here.'

Decima looks at me quizzically. I raise an eyebrow. A glint of recognition and she falls in. We see Pam and the dogs to the door. Decima hates goodbyes as much as I do. She doesn't make a fuss of them. There is also the little question of our minds being on other things. But as soon as the door is closed, she crumbles. I hold her and let the tears fall.

'Er, there's one thing…' Here goes. 'The thing is, Decima. We've discussed it. Astrid, Alice, Patrick and I…'

She stiffens and jerks her head up. 'Discussed what? I knew something was going on between you.'

I put my hand on her shoulder and cup her newly blossomed cheek in my hand, 'I'm going to be away for a long time.' I kiss her softly on the lips.

'You might as well leave me. Everybody else has.'

'Will you come?'

'What? Where? To England? How can I, I'm dead!'

'Astrid has arranged for some, er, doctoring of your passport.'

'Are you serious? To your castle?' She pulls away from me.

'Don't get too excited, it's not what you think but there are a few perks. The thing is, I truly need your help. I have a big fight on my hands with this Erica woman.'

'Oh yes, the tiara tart,' she smiles.

'And who is better at fighting with words than you? Would you be willing to help me? It could take a while, weeks, months, it's impossible to say but er… Look, if it comes to it, we could ship Twinkle and Barney out. There's a quarantine, but you'd have them every day, we could go for long walks, the Sussex downs are sensational for walks, and the beaches aren't too far away.'

She smiles, 'And a fight. I'll get my passport. I do think it's in the bedroom,' she says, pulling me by the hand.

'Now, where did I put it?' She runs her hands up and down my back. We fall onto the bed and make love like we've never, ever made love before.

17

Remembering Josh

Alice

I've finally accepted that Josh did not escape the fire, and we will never see him again. Why he was at the Tower late that night we'll never know, but it wasn't unusual for him to work at odd hours on his special effects ideas. The security guard who passed him going into the Tower about an hour before the explosion never saw him leave. There is no record of him being among the injured who were treated on site, nor any of those admitted to hospital. His phone number goes unanswered. The forensic laboratory have so far been unable to identify any of the cremated remains, but all the evidence points to Josh having perished together with Decima and the unfortunate cleaning lady, Marla Carrera.

Those of us who know that Decima has in fact survived are wondering who the remains of the third person belong to. Nobody has been reported missing, but in a huge building like the Tower it's more than likely there were other people there at the time whose disappearance has not been reported.

Josh's son and daughter are making their own arrangements for a private memorial service, family only, so we are having a quiet ceremony here to say goodbye to him. Decima is dressed in black, with a lacy veil draped over her head.

We set up a table beneath a tulip tree in the garden, place a photo of Josh in the center, with a bowl of white roses and a candle each side, and take it in turns to say how we remember him.

Sean steps forward to speak about how thoughtful Josh was, how you could always go to him if you had a problem and he'd take all the time in the world to listen and help you sort it out. 'Josh was like your favorite uncle,' he says. 'Always with a smile and a kind word.' He gives a little bow to the photo and backs away slowly with his head hanging.

'Obviously Ramon is unable to be here in person, but he is in spirit, and has sent a message he wants me to read out,' says Cory.

'Josh, you were one hell of a guy, a true genius, and it was a privilege to have worked with you. Rest easy, big man.'

Decima is sobbing into her hands.

'What can I say, Josh?' says Cory. 'You did not only create the greatest ever special effects; you were the best mentor anybody could hope for. I owe you everything for your patience, willingness to give your time and share your expertise. You were not just a colleague, you were a friend, and we are all going to miss you. Godspeed.'

Decima is wailing. She's collapsed onto Sean, who is awkwardly trying to hold her up by her arms without touching her body.

'Decima?' asks Cory. 'Do you want to say something?' He goes to her side and supports her as she lurches towards the table.

'Waieeeeeee,' she shrieks. 'Josh, my great big beautiful bear.' She throws herself at the table, picks up the photo and kisses it wildly. Cory grabs the table just in time to stop it falling over, trying to hold Decima up at the same time.

She presses the photo to her face and howls, then raises her face to the sky and screams 'Don't leave me here Josh. Come back! You cannot be dead. You're my everything! I want to die!' She flings herself to the ground and kicks her legs up and down, jamming her fist into her mouth and biting her knuckles. Cory kneels beside her and takes her into his arms, stroking her hair and rocking her back and forwards until her screams fade into sobs.

'Come on,' he croons. 'Josh would hate to see you like this. Be a big girl for him.' He lifts her to her feet and holds her close. She sniffs and smears away her tears and smudges of mascara, still clutching the soggy photo of Josh.

I take it very gently from her hand and prop it back up on the table.

'When I was at my lowest, you found me, Josh, and you comforted me. I will always remember your kindness.'

I also remember that he betrayed me to Decima, but I push that from my mind.

'You were the glue that held us together, the magician who made the programme what it was, the shoulder to weep on, the quiet voice to calm nerves, the twinkling eyes full of fun. You were wise, and wonderful and we will all miss you very much. If you are looking down on us from up there, here is something for you, which comes with my love.'

I point at the table, and the roses begin to blush from white to pink, deepening in color until they are crimson. The photo expands, enlarging itself until it is life-sized, and a great smile appears on Josh's face. The candles send spirals of silver smoke into the air, hovering over the table and filling the air with the sound of thunderous bells ringing out.

At first everybody gasps. We stand there watching until the smoke and noise fade out, and the photo returns to its original size.

'What did I just see there with my own eyes?' mutters Sean. 'Unbelievable.'

'Yeah,' Cory says. 'That was quite something. Josh would have liked that.'

Decima is still staring at the table. I take the photo and hand it to her.

'Alice,' she whispers hoarsely. She reaches out and puts her arms around me, pulling me close. 'Will you ever stop amazing me?'

18

Fergus & James' box of tricks

Decima

Astrid thinks I should go to England which only makes me want to stay more. We're on the old swing sofa at the shady end of the garden, shelling peas. The combination of the rhythmic squeak of the swing, the pop of peas and the floral cushions warm on my bare thighs remind me of childhood summers. Before my real parents were taken away from me. This is the feeling of home. This whole place has wrapped itself tight around me, holding me warm and safe and I don't want to leave.

'Your dogs are settled and happy, Decima – now it's time for you to be settled and happy.'

A breeze picks up out of nowhere and ripples the leaf shadows that dapple the lawn. 'I am. I'm settled here now. I don't want to lose you and, and – Patrick. Alice. Sean I can do without…'

We laugh. I'm sure I hear a snigger coming from Astrid's cat, curled up under the shade of the bushes.

'Shall I tell you what the answer is to that?'

'Yes, Astrid. Please.'

'No matter what the situation, there's always a twister, a turn-about, you can take. If you look hard enough. Whatever it is. Even presumed dead and locked away like this.' She holds up a pea shell and pops it. 'Whufff! Turn it around. There you go! And you know what? That's pure energy right there. Power for yourself.'

In one movement, her thumb slices out the row of peas into the bowl.

'But,' she continues, picking a pea from the bowl and popping it in her mouth, 'the real power comes when you stop thinking about yourself so much my dear. The more you think about others, the more you help others, the less bother you'll be to yourself. Cory needs you. That's his gift to you. That's all any of us want. To be needed. So there's your answer.'

'I'm sorry, Astrid, but Cory, of all people, has never needed anyone. He's the most self-contained guy on the planet.'

'Don't you be so sure, my dear.'

'But… *years?* All this time here, building up my career. Wasted. I'd be a complete nobody in England. What'll I do?'

'You'll be safe.'

'I need more than *safe,* Astrid. I'm safe here with you aren't I. I'm a career woman, a famous TV presenter, I can't simply *stop* and disappear… When the news does come out that I'm alive, my stats are going to go through the roof. I can start up again. Not CGO TV naturally, another station. A national station even…'

'Why is fame so important to you?'

'It's not. I'm so over that.'

'It doesn't sound like it to me. Why did you go into it in the first place?'

'Chance. It was a chance opportunity. After Lorelei was fired. But I wanted it. Oh, I wanted it.'

'Why?'

'To get the respect I deserve I suppose.'

'What does respect mean? Importance. What does importance mean? Power over others. That you're somehow better than them.'

'But I'm not!'

'Exactly,' she beams. 'That's where it breaks down.'

The cat strolls over and jumps up. It looks at me with a lizardy glint, and, I swear it, a wink, turns a few times and settles on my lap.

Later that day I'm upstairs, resting and thinking about Astrid's words. Cory's kiss on my doorstep was a big shock. First, because it happened at all. We never kiss. Second, because I enjoyed it. I know he only did that to shut me up. But it wasn't bad and then when we explored it more, a lot more, later on. Well…! We were like a straight couple there, in my bed, in my house, that day. He made love to me. *We* made love. The love wasn't he or I, it was between us. It felt real. If we're both stuck in England… in his bed – in his bed in his castle – it will be a 4-poster, with curtains, right? Where would it go from there?

Suddenly Astrid is there, at the end of my bed. I wish these witchy people wouldn't do that.

'Sorry to interrupt your rest. There's been a hitch. We need you downstairs now, and please bring your passport. Fergus and James has arrived.'

'Who?'

'He dropped by on his way to the AI Conference over in Hidden Springs…'

'And who's James.'

'James is Fergus too, he's half Polish, half Scottish,' she said as if that explained it. She's bustling about my room, Alice's room, opening, and closing drawers.

'What are you looking for?'

'Patrick thought your passport might arouse suspicion, you are looking so different now, so he asked Fergus and James to stop by to er, manipulate your photo a little. But when he found out that you were MPD…'

'MP what?'

'Missing Presumed Dead. He said that was a whole lot more complicated.'

'It's here…' I slide it out from beneath my pillow and hand it over. Tell the whole world about me, why don't you?'

'Oh the Prof is nothing to worry about, he's rarely in this realm, he'll be gone in a puff of smoke before nightfall. It's as well we were cautious. Laser engravings, signatures, holograms, polycarbonate plastics, Fergus and James is your man, even with AI. But there's nothing he can do with an MPD. The FBI will instantly steel-door you.'

'So I'd be declared alive.'

'In moments, yes. '

'And then I'll be all over the news.'

'Immediately. As you well know, there are journos hanging about at every airport in the world, hoping for exactly those kinds of scoops.'

'And so then Gauld will track me down and I'll be dead. For real.'

'Er well...'

'That's it then. I can't go.'

'That's why he's here. We need your passport and your nose, downstairs now. He's not sure it'll work but he's willing to give it a try.'

Suddenly this place doesn't feel so cozy. Any doubts I had have disappeared. Whatever, whoever, this Fergus and James is, if he can get me out of here, I'm in.

As soon as I reach the bottom of the stairs, a riot of color leaps towards me, fist stretched out before him.

'Fergus and James, my pleasure,' he mumbles, 'But call me Fergus, do do do.'

I go in for the fist bump, but before I get there, in one swift sleight of hand, he's taken my passport from my other hand and is on the other side of the room. It was kind of rude. Really rude actually, but impressive.

I glance at Astrid and Patrick, sitting side by side like proud parents waiting for the show to begin. 'Everybody ready?' Fergus straightens to full height and raises both arms like a conductor. With corkscrew hair frothing out of a multi-colored, crochet hat, he's a crazy alright. His eyes shine at me through tiny bi-focal glasses balanced at the end of his, I have to say, magnificent schnoz of a nose.

I'm only permitted to be present at this secret ceremony, he tells me, because he can't proceed without my nose being there in person. After I've signed some kind of witchy official secrets act, he holds my passport between the palms of his hands and instructs me to step forwards. I stand in front of him and he mutters and mumbles for what seems like forever.

I glance over at the expectant faces of Astrid and Patrick flickering in the candlelight.

Eventually, it happens. He opens his palms out and my passport wobbles into the air. He darts forward, grabs at my nose, pinches it tight and holds his hand over my mouth. Blood rushes to my head. My throat gets tighter until I'm writhing and squealing. He lets go. The gasp that comes out of me is threaded with wisps of inky blue streaks. I scream. More inky air vomits out of my mouth, swirls around the spinning passport and starts threading itself between the covers. When the last of it has gone, the passport stops spinning and lands with a loud slap at my feet. I reach to pick it up, but Patrick springs forward and gets there first.

'That'll be all,' he tucks my passport into his waistcoat inner pocket and nods at Astrid. She steps forward, takes my arm like I'm some kind of criminal and escorts me away, explaining that Patrick will keep it safe and 'active'. The first time it's opened must be for the airport inspection or the whole thing could fail.

19

How dare they!

Decima

I'm fuming! This is what being dead is like. Cory… *Cory* is trusted with my, *my* identity, above *me*.

I don't see my passport again until we're in the Departures queue.

When he finally hands it over, I take it with a huffy snatch. We shuffle forwards in line. My heart beats louder. If this goes wrong I'll be all over the news in no time.

'Decima Gauld fake death!'

'She's alive!'

'Decima Gauld caught escaping the country.'

What would happen after that plays over and over in my head like some straight-to-video B movie. My father's goons grab their guns and race out to their cars to hunt me down and finish me off.

We're nearly at the front of the queue. I feel guilty as charged and know one hundred percent it's all over my face.

'Small talk,' I hiss. 'Make small talk now.'

Cory doesn't look up.

I try to get some bland conversation going. 'I was in London not so long ago. Fabienne took me to this restaurant on the river. Do you remember her? I wonder what happened to…'

'We're not going to London,' he snaps. 'Sussex is closer to France than London.'

'I mean, off the scale, expense account, incredible restaurant. And I'd only arrived a few hours earlier. First Class.'

'Get ready to slum it then. None of us are on the Dubai dollar any longer.'

The queue ahead disappears and he's at the desk. He retrieves his passport with a nod and walks away without a glance back.

We have agreed that if I'm caught, I'm on my own. No matter what happens to me, he needs to get to the UK to sort out all that goes with a death in the family and a complicated inheritance.

Here goes.

I take a deep breath, approach the desk and hand over my passport. He looks up at me. Looks down. Looks up again, stares into my eyes. Taps something into the screen.

He's handing it back. I can't believe it.

'Have a good trip Miss Archer.'

I open my mouth to correct him, close it again quickly

and hurry off to find Cory. What the…?

'What? *What?*' I hiss.

'Shush.' He grips my arm. We dodge through the retail stores at a fast clip and don't stop until we're at the Gate.

The stop-start queue to get to our seats takes forever. The plane is horribly full and we're right at the back. If we'd turned left, we'd be settled in by now with champagne, six types of canape and endless hot towels.

'It *worked*,' Cory whispers, fumbling for his seatbelt, 'We're on our way.'

I sit motionless, erect, too incensed to let any words out of my mouth in case I lose control and blow my cover.

I open my passport, or, should I say, *Alice's* passport. Yes, there's her name and there's my photo.

I examine the nose, looking for the join, and think back to that afternoon with Fergus & James. Why didn't I question why he wanted my nose when my nose was, *of course*, already on my passport? When that's about the only thing that hasn't changed about face? He must have switched my passport for Alice's in those first few moments.

As for Astrid. Jennifer Anniston indeed! What a trusting fool I was. I thought we were getting closer and closer, I was ready to be adopted for real, when all the while she was molding my face into a cheap copy of her own daughter. Screwed up or what?

'All that *Now don't open your passport until you're through…*

RUBBISH, ' I mutter, clicking in my seatbelt with as much strop as I can muster. 'It's a slap in the face, Cory. And it's not even my face.'

'Keep your voice down.' Cory puts on an eye mask, crosses his arms and tightens his jaw. Despite my mood, I can't help but giggle to myself at the sight of him. He must be scared of flying.

I take a moment to study Lord Cholmondeley of Trenmaddick and wonder what's going on inside that enigmatic mind of his.

Why do you want me to be with you so badly, Cory? Because you need a Rottweiler for Erica? Or because you want us to be together? Or am I nothing more than your Alice lookalike? Is that why you made love to me so tenderly with those oh so soft, caresses and kisses?

Have you been faking the free and easy hipster persona I've known all this time? Or are you still the laid-back possession-hater, now on your way to inherit a fortune? Were you able to play with all that freedom because you always knew there was a title and property waiting for you one day?

I sigh. It's hard to come to terms with this. I've never met a more genuine guy in my life. But then, here we are, both in the same weird kind of boat. Neither of us is who we're supposed to be or who we think we are.

My eyes, and then a hand, strays to his passport sticking out from his seat flap.

Lord Cornelius Ablett Cholmondeley... Cornelius!

No Mr. But Lord. There it is in black and white. The old faker. He's the real deal, isn't he. For reasons I'll never understand, Cholmondeley is pronounced Chumley. I go to the back page. In Case of Emergency, contact Jonathan Cholmondeley… so they're not that estranged then. Or weren't. This is nearly ten years old. Whoa here's the address…

Trenmaddick
Mount Caburn
Glynde
Sussex BE9 2JJ

Cory sits up.

'Why aren't we moving?' He takes off his mask and looks up at a steward behind us. I have just enough time to hide his passport beneath a magazine before he turns back.

'How should I know?'

'I've never felt so tense.'

The captain announces there'll be a delay to take-off. Due to unforeseen circumstances.

'*Unforeseen circumstances.* That'll be me, then,' I whisper.

Cory puts a hand on my knee. 'Whatever happens,' he says, kissing me tenderly on the neck. 'Please know that I really didn't want to do this trip without you.'

It feels warm and comforting but I shrug him off.

Who knows what's genuine and what's fake anymore?

I don't even know who I am and who I'm not. My passport here, which has nothing to do with me, is the living proof. I flip through to the photo. Who came first? Alice with Decima's nose or Decima with Alice's face? I study it closely, twisting it around in the light, looking for the join. There is none, Fergus and James have pulled it off it seems. If I'm not hauled off the plane now, what if I'm stopped at the other end? Stealing and defacing a passport has to be jail. I can't google it. If I'm dragged out of the immigration queue and taken into custody, my phone history is the first place they'll look. I have no choice but to be Alice Archer now until we're out the other side.

If I get that far.

I swallow hard and wait for the tap on my shoulder.

20

The whole caboodle

Cory

Because of the delay, by the time we find a taxi and reach the village it's gone midnight. By village I mean a couple of bends in the road with a few cottages scattered about. A few of them belong to the Estate. To me now I suppose.

I haven't taken it all in yet. I must protect what's legally mine, but I've worked so hard to not be a victim of my own possessions and here's the whole caboodle, tumbling towards me at a rate of knots.

After the signpost for the heath and the pub, I see the familiar green lights of the BP service station ahead. We slow down. I had planned for us to go to The Sportsman first. I've no idea what's going to greet us at Tremaddick, and I wanted to get the latest from Simon the manager. He knows everything that happens around here before people know it themselves most of the time. As it's so late, Simon has gone to bed and we have no option but to go straight to Tremaddick.

The driver should have his indicator on by now.

I reach forward ready to direct him up the invisible, sharp left, side-road but sit back again when I see his SatNav line bending at the correct spot. He's a cab driver. A cab driver with SatNav. Relax Cory. Relax, man. Om mani padmi hum. Om mani…

I can sense Decima's excitement.

'Not far now.' I rest a hand gently on her knee.

I'm so glad she's here. Back on the plane, the thought that I might have had to do this without her by my side was awful. I've never in my life felt such a need for somebody who might be snatched away from me at any moment. Even looking at her, perhaps for the last time in weeks, months, was all too much. Thank goodness I had my eye mask to hand. Instead of gazing at who I might be about to lose, I lost myself in darkness. I've worked damned hard over the years nurturing my independence, I have had no need of anybody. Ever. That's the safest way to live. The ultimate. I had the whole flight to examine those alien feelings of extreme need for another person. By the time we landed I was pretty sure I knew what was going on, deep down, though I am in no way ready to accept it. Practically, I really do need Decima's help to deal with this Erica woman. That's enough analyzing for now. But Jonty's death is an irony not lost on me. I've been set free from myself. Being a twin is complicated, no matter what your relationship. As much as Decima has had her identity changed by circumstance, so have I. I can now be with another, heart and soul, as I could never be with my twin.

We turn into the single track lane.

'What if a car comes the other way?' says Decima.

'That won't happen,' I squeeze her hand. She strokes my finger. Electricity charges through me.

What was that? Come on Cory, speak honestly to yourself at least. Love is certainly a strange beast isn't it. When Sean fell for Alice, I got it. I had strong feelings of affection for her too. But when he became obsessed, I secretly put it down to some kind of Midsummer Night's Dream insanity. But that's not it at all, is it. Falling in love is so much quieter than that, and, in your own head, so much louder at the same time. As simple as breathing. A knowing. Something you know. And if you both know. Then, bingo.

Too soon to call? My emotions are all over the place. My first task now is to not frighten her away. Decima has had enough shocks lately, and there are a good few more to come when she sees where she'll be living for the coming days.

We turn right again into open fields, the track now has a single rail fence on each side. The rent from this farmland kept Jonathan going, just about. But not quite enough in the style he would have wished.

After a mile or so, we turn sharply left into a hairpin bend up a steep slope. The grass in the middle is wider than the tyre tracks now. The driver selects a lower gear and the engine grumbles.

This is it. I feel a horrible sense of dread. I so do hope it's not going to be too complicated. At least he had the wisdom to die that night Alice and I visited before she could get a ring on him.

We pull up. Decima is staring intently out of the window into the blackness.

Here we go.

'Enjoy your stay, Sir,' are the taxi driver's parting words. 'I'm sorry for your loss.'

'We'll try to,' I say steadily and evenly and put a £10.00 tip into his hand. I'm shocked that this taxi driver, who covers the whole of Sussex area, knows what happened to Jonty. A timely reminder that everyone around these parts knows more about you than you think. Everything we do will be under intense scrutiny, all eyes will be on us, even if they're averted. Especially if they're averted.

21

First impressions

Decima

We're high up on some kind of hill in the literal middle of nowhere and a nasty wind is whipping my hair into my face. I switch on my phone torch and shine it up at the great shadow of the building in front of us to see the largest door I've ever seen.

Whilst Cory fumbles for keys, I go to take a closer look. Blackened dark wood panels, rotten and splintered, are studded all over with metal bolts. Halfway down, at about my eye-level, there's a great hole with a circle at the top, widening out at the bottom, like a cartoon keyhole.

I nod at Cory's little black man-bag, 'If you have a key for this in there, then you're Mary Poppins.'

'This isn't it,' he says crisply, picking up cases. I follow him around to the side of the building.

'Nobody's used that door since the Plantagenets. Or the great hall for that matter. Impressive back in the day, but wholly impractical. Useless really.'

We pass walls covered in vegetation. Through the ivy I make out a few turreted windows. I can't be sure in the dark but do they even have any glass in them? At the back of this great square building is an overgrown field that must have been lawns at one time, bordered by high trees, rustling in the wind. We follow the wall, until we reach a narrow opening. We turn right and squeeze through a tight passage that ends in a flimsy, light blue door. After some fumbling with the keys, we're inside.

I follow Cory down a long, thin corridor to a dingy room with peeling brown wallpaper and high ceilings. It smells of burnt toast. In the middle is a yellow formica table and chairs. Perched on top of an old fridge-freezer is a microwave oven that's seen better days. An old flowery sofa and matching armchair face an enormous TV screen and a tiny electric bar fire.

'I thought your brother lived in a castle not a slum?'

'The truth of it is, Decima, he lived at the pub. His home was a barstool. Boring the socks off anybody who would listen to him. I don't know how Simon put up with him for so long.'

Cory looks like he's going to burst into tears. He's crestfallen. Ashamed. I feel for him. We're both exhausted. On the table is a Planet Organic shopping bag and an empty 4-carton of Krispy Kremes. There are plates and mugs piled into a yellow plastic bowl in the sink. On the draining board are empty Coke cans, a half-full Bacardi bottle and black trash bags. Heavy blue velvet curtains are half-drawn across a huge pair of frosted windows. Countless mini pots of herbs in plastic containers are lined up on the kitchen units, surrounded by random piles of plates, mugs and bowls.

He bends down and holds his hand over the two black bars of the electric fire.

'Well, either Jonty has come back from the dead, or we appear to have an unwelcome visitor.'

I put my hand next to his and feel the heat.

Cory switches the fire back on. We sit on the sofa and huddle over it until we're warm enough to lean back and wrap ourselves around each other.

22

The woman in white

Decima

I'm woken by a scream. I look up to see this… thing …
this apparition, like a great white shark, hovering over us.
Black panda eyes peer out through a tangle of bleached
white hair. Its face is as white as its robe. I freak the freak
right out. I'm not familiar with ghost stories but even I
have heard of the woman in white.

It waves its arms wildly, flicking its hands at us and
shrieking.

'Who on earth are YOU? What are you doing here?
Get out, get OUT, GET OUT of here. NOW!'

I grab hold of Cory. It freezes in its tracks and fixes
Cory with a still, silent stare. It looks from Cory to me
and back again. Cory holds me closer. Through all the
craziness of the moment I feel a warm glow inside.
Protection feels good.

It doesn't pounce but, with a whimpering cry, turns
and runs to the sink, picks up a milk pan, opens the fridge
and crouches behind the door. This woman is so broad

we can still see everything except her face. I notice the yellow stains on her nightgown. Egg?

Cory goes over and reaches out an arm. 'Steady now, you don't want to lose the baby.'

With a shriek of terror, she slams the fridge shut, runs to the window and hides behind the curtains.

'Jonty!' says the lump from behind the curtain. 'Jonty you're DEAD Jonty! Oh my, oh my, I cannot believe this is happening… and who is SHE… Not dead five minutes and pulled already. Typical. *Typical…* '

Cory strides across the room and rips the curtain back. She screams and scuttles back to the fridge.

Cory follows.

She switches her attention to me. She looks at me, at Cory, then back to me on the sofa.

'Ah. Ahhhhh! I know who you are,' she whispers. 'I know exactly who you are. I know what you're here for. Ah yes yes yes...' She straightens to full height, puts her hand on her great belly, smirks and says. 'Well, you're too late mate. You're not gettin any of it. Now get out. Get outta my house before I call the cops.'

'Now there's no need for that.'

'What do you think you're playing at?' she snarls. 'Turning up like this when it's all over.'

'I think you know the answer to that, Erica,' Cory says formally.

'To grab what you can, isn't it. You were the one who ran away… ran away like the weedy little bro you are.'

'I grew up,' Cory explains unnecessarily with a casual shrug.

With a curl of her top lip, she tucks the milk pan under her arm and takes out a cigarette. We watch her light up, take a deep drag and blow it out noisily.

'Left all of this for Jonty to look after didn't you.'

'And hasn't he done *that* well,' I say.

She rolls her eyes over me, up and down and up again. 'What makes you think you can waltz in and take it all back. Well you're too late. See? Too late…'

I hold her stare in a glare-off. I win. She circles Cory. He watches her. Calm to the point of expressionless.

This will be interesting. Cory doesn't do conflict. He'll let her go on and on and then turn it around with the fewest of words.

The less he reacts the more annoyed she will get. I feel a twang of empathy. I know that feeling.

'Put that down now,' he says calmly.

She raises her arm. 'Now. NOW! Who do you think you are telling me what to do? Lord of the manor? Ha! Well you're too late there matey. Oh Oh…' she spreads her legs and bends forward in pain and cradles her bump.

Oh no don't let her give birth.

Copying Cory, I take a deep breath, step forward and say, calm as anything, 'You heard him. You're trespassing. You have to leave.'

Her eyebrows shoot up. She stands straight and faces me eyeball to eyeball. 'This,' she pokes a finger at my chest, 'lady,' poke, 'is none of your business.'

'No, it's his.' I wave my arm around at all the miserable clutter…. 'All of this. *His.* Understand?'

'Look,' Cory interrupts softly. 'We're going to leave you here now, OK? You can stay here for the time being.'

'Three days. We'll give you three days,' I add quickly, giving Cory a look. She's a user. Give this type a hint of an advantage and she'll pick it up and run with it. She touches her bump and leans forward, breathing heavily.

'Get your things together, sort yourself out,' says Cory. 'He's gone, I know that must be hard for you when you were so close to marrying him in hospital.'

'Eh?'

'I know, Erica. I was there with Jonty that night. You saw me. Remember?'

Something dawns on her. She grabs a chunk of her hair and twirls it around one finger.

'I saw it all. That was a very fetching tiara you were wearing.'

It's my turn to look surprised. I shoot Cory a look. How could he have known that?

She shuffles to the fridge. I think she's going to hide behind the door again, but a raised hand appears. Something flies through the air and lands on my shoulder. It doesn't hurt but collapses in on me. I reach up to touch this sticky mess when another one flies towards me. Eggs! And another. She has a whole box of twelve in her hand now and launches them at me one by one.

Cory loses it. He shrieks at her to calm down.

She stands looking from Cory to the egg box and back to Cory again. 'Jonty, oh Jonty…' She falls onto him and bursts into tears.

He disentangles himself and escorts her to the table. With a great noisy snort she puts down the egg box and sinks heavily, legs apart, onto a chair.

'We need to sort this out, that much is clear.' Cory goes to the sink and gets her a glass of water.

'Yes, you need to leave,' I say.

'*You* need to leave, woman,' she says, gulping down the water. 'I have rights.'

'You do,' says Cory. 'You'll get housed somewhere far nicer than here. Somewhere warm. With heating. And proper windows. Close to the shops,' he says gently.

I can see her mind whirring.

She sits up straight. 'What you talking about. This place is mine now. It belongs to me, you hear?'

She stares at him. Her face freezes. 'You do look like him don't you? It's uncanny.' and she bursts into tears again. Cory looks offended. Insulted. Confused. She got him on the back foot there. He doesn't know what to do. He's lost for words. He's stammering. Maybe she really did love Jonty?

It's time for me to step in. My prime role on *The Bitch's Hour* was interrogation. I'd give the guests a sense of security. A false sense of security. Then drop in the killer question when they were least expecting it. It's an art. And I'm the best in the business. I puff out my chest, lean across the table and whisper into her face.

'This. Isn't your home. You have. To. Leave.'

She leaps up. Shiny pink nails are coming for my eyes. I reciprocate, acrylic against acrylic.

Cory pulls me back.

'Look here. If we have to go the legal route, that's what we'll do Erica. How's that? I'll be seeing quite a bit of my lawyers in the coming weeks. With the official switch of everything into my name. I'm sure we can draw up some kind of temporary contract. You won't be out on the street in any case.'

She is slumped on the table. I can see Cory has weakened already.

'It'll cost you,' I say. 'Every day you are here from now on we are going to be charging you rent. What do you think Cory, for a house this size? What can your hot Trust Fund lawyers get out of her. It might be useful income until we sell. What do you reckon? How many bedrooms? 12? £1,000 a week? Cheap at the price. There you go, Erica. Dirt cheap. Just like you.'

23

The Sportsman

Cory

'Who needs a castle when there are pubs?' Decima stops bouncing on the 4-poster for a moment to slot Digby in between the snow white sheets.

'My dear departed brother's sentiment entirely.'

She turns and grins. 'He's the dear departed now is he?'

'When we came into the bar, I fully expected to see him perched as always on his corner stool. It did give me a jolt.'

I frown at the half-bald, half-burnt, bear taking up the all-important center of our bed. I'm an easy-going chap but we'll have to talk about this mangy love-blocker at some point. For now, it's a joy to see her happy. I cross the room, pull back the curtain and peer out at the rain. It's so dark it could be evening already.

'I only hope I can get the paperwork sorted out quickly.'

'Then what?'

'Get it on the market pronto.'

'All of it?'

'It's not much use to us, is it?'

'You have no sentiment, Cory. It's been in your family forever.'

'Yes, it has. Hundreds of years of bad luck. Don't worry, it's not going anywhere soon. You'll have plenty of time to get to know the place. The land and the cottages will go quickly but castles tend to linger on estate agents' books for years. Someone will want it. Eventually.'

'Like, Erica.'

'Having Jonty's child out of wedlock doesn't entitle her to anything.'

'She seems to think it does.'

'Well we'll see about that. Where's the WiFi code?'

I set my phone up and click through.

'Still no news. I really should have had a copy of the Will by now.'

'Don't we have to sit in a room whilst some crusty old lawyer reads it out?'

'Only in old movies. The world has moved on since then. I nearly choked when you told Erica our lawyers were hot. That couldn't be further from the truth. He's a hopeless twat. Been with the family for decades. Always has been. I'll give him a call when we've settled in.

'Any news from home?'

'Sean has checked in on WhatsApp. He has a new song.'

'So what's new. Pam?'

I find Pam's latest Instagram reel, our agreed way of communicating from Twinkle and Barney to Decima. 'There you go…' I hand my phone over. She cuddles Digby and curls up with the screen. I don't know what she's missing more, her phone or her dogs.

I leave her to it and take a shower. When it's my turn for the phone again, Ramon has popped up in the group, congratulating Sean on his new song. Our WhatsApp group is guys only. A much-needed release in the past. I carefully consider my words before speaking. I don't want her scrolling through our past messages.

'There's a message from Ramon too.'

'How's he doing?'

Wrapped in a towel, I sit on the edge of the bed and scroll quickly through his long message.

'Difficult to say. He says he's enjoying himself, but it's hard work. Really hard work making a movie. I think that's come as a bit of a shock.' I quickly scan a big chunk of text about his visit to the kisaeng house. I'll read that later.

'Send him my love. When do I get the tour?'

'The tour? Oh, the rest of the castle. Yes we'll do that this afternoon if you like. Though the weather is pretty awful.'

'How about tomorrow?' She grabs my hand and pulls

me backwards.

'I dare say it'll all still be there tomorrow,' I say, returning her kisses. Reaching behind her back, I gently slide her bear out of the sheets and drop him onto the floor.

24

The guided tour

Decima

A twist in the road and there in the distance is Tremaddick, rising out of the mist like Dracula's castle.

The cab drops us off and, hunched over against the weather, we head for the back door. The wind hasn't let up, blowing the rain sideways into our faces.

'As you can see,' Cory shouts above the wind, 'nobody's lived here for donkey's years.'

'Er, except Jonty.'

'Technically I suppose. He slept in the kitchen but he really did live at the pub. Had all his meals there. And drinks, more to the point. Poor Simon must be feeling the pinch badly.'

'How long has it been like this?'

'Forever. It started crumbling away soon after World War II.'

'So where did you grow up?'

'We lived in a cottage on the Estate. This has been nothing but a folly forever.'

'What happened to your parents?'

'They died.' He says in such a way as to not invite any more questions.

Give it time.

At the back, we reach a crumbling fountain with some kind of cream cherub statue holding a fish. The great trees fringing the field sway in the wind like they're going to bend right over.

'There are no cars here,' I say with relief. 'She must be out.'

'Maybe she's decided to leave.'

'I doubt that.'

The grounds go on forever, sloping down on one side to a walled garden and a long, low rusting greenhouse. I look up at the ruin and wonder if it's even safe to go in. I have to trust him on that. Cory knows about old buildings more than I do. I guess it's been here for hundreds of years without falling down.

'OK let's get the tour over with. Follow me.'

'You alright?' I touch his arm. He doesn't reply.

We proceed cautiously, like Erica might be waiting around the next corner ready to pounce. One creepy, sad room leads to the next. The smell of mold and damp is overwhelming. A few bits of flimsy old furniture remain, ugly wing-back armchairs like you see in hospitals, peppered with random, sad, flat cushions. Yellowed polystyrene ceiling tiles that have lost their grip are scattered everywhere, swirly wallpaper peels from crumbling walls.

Before it became derelict, it was some kind of a recuperation home for patients back from the war, he tells me. We reach a solid oak door.

'The Grand Hall,' he stands back and invites me to enter first.

It must have been. Once. The roof is open to the elements. The wind howls, blowing in gusts of rain. The brick walls are covered in moss. On the right, what glass remains on a long row of turreted windows is cracked and streaked with bird droppings.

Cory crosses to a great stone fireplace, so big you can walk inside. Except you can't because there's a horrible, dusty, dried flower and feather arrangement in the grate.

He touches the coat of arms in the center of the mantle and turns to me.

'See how meaningless it all is now?'

'It meant something once, Cory.'

He gives me a strange look. If only for fairytales I think. Oh for a camera. I take a mental image of my lover standing there, one hand on his family crest. His fine black hair slicked back by the rain, looking every bit the fairytale prince.

'Not today. Not now. This is what Jonty was trying to hold onto. So very sad, don't you think? Like grasping at air.'

I'm beginning to understand why he shies off possessions. On our way out we pass a bureau made of heavily carved black wood. It's massive but dwarfed by the size of the room. On the surface, propped up on a stand, is a solitary plate decorated with a hunting scene. I wonder who put it there? His parents?

'It'll be behind you soon,' I say softly.

'To be fair, this is not Jonty's fault.' He leads me back the way we came, through to another wing. 'Erica is right. I was the one who ran away.'

'Don't be hard on yourself.'

'There's something I want you to see, come.'

After several more corridors, we climb up a twisting stone staircase. And I mean climb. It's so steep I have to hold on to each step in front for dear life. We emerge on the tower roof. I put my umbrella up but the wind takes it. Braving the rain, I walk to the turreted edge and look out at the view.

The weather reminds me of our walks with the dogs, when we first got together, one on one. When we first realized something was happening between us, beyond my using his body for my own pleasure. I feel so ashamed of that now. I feel ashamed of so much.

We stand close. Then closer. I peer down to the courtyard below, a square of weeds and grass.

'Up. Up. Always look up,' he whispers, gesturing over the misty sweep of hills and forest. 'On a clear day you can see the sea. I promise.'

We get closer. I feel his arms around me. The jacket he's wearing smells of liquorice and library. A library full of dusty old books. I breathe him in. My breath turns into a sigh. My sigh to a moan.

He pulls me in tighter and tips my face towards his. We kiss.

'Don't you see,' he whispers. 'Bricks, mortar, land. Land doesn't belong to anybody. Jonty was clutching at air. Money is security, nothing else. A roof above your head is all you need. Security is poppycock. Insecurity, change, is all there is. What will last is us, Decima. You. Me. Together.'

We kiss again. And again. Long, slow, lingering kisses. Kisses that don't lead anywhere because we're already there. All we want in each other is fulfilled. Deepened. Together as one.

'Let's go home.'

'Let's go home, Decima.'

'Together.'

'Before we do…' he pulls away from me, adjusts his jacket, and gets down on one knee.

25

Blossoms

Alice

Years from now I will look back at the photos from the front page of the Hawk Bay City Herald featuring the opening of Blossoms.

The main photo shows Mrs Blossom symbolically handing me the keys. (In fact we have been working inside the shop for almost two months, since she first agreed to sell it to me.)

In a second, smaller photo, my parents stand behind Sean and myself, each with their hands on our shoulders. The caption reads: 'New owner Miss Alice Archer and her fiancé Sean Mahey, with Miss Archer's parents, Astrid and Patrick Archer.'

We are all smiling, except for Sean who decided instead to pull a goofy face which makes me laugh when I look at it now.

A third photo shows me hanging the crystal wind chimes, and the newspaper tells the tale of how Mrs Blossom's gift led to me buying her shop.

Finally there's Sean and his skateboard, with a banner

streaming from the back, a replica of the shop sign.

Yesterday it rained all day. The streets were flooded and the wind was gusting, and I thought it couldn't be worse weather for opening. After a restless night, when I swung from certainty the shop would be a success and the overwhelming fear that I was making a crazy mistake, this morning the sun came out as if by its own magic.

We are all there very early to remove the screens around the building and reveal the new facade. The sunrise highlights the gold lettering which Sean has painted so carefully, so it glows against the green background. My father delivers our first crop of plants, lovingly and magically grown by my mother, and Shelley creates a glorious display in every color of the rainbow, arranged in recycled metallic pots on the shelves and on the pavement beside the door. When the sun strikes the pots, they shine like silver, and the smell of the various flowers blends into the most glorious perfume. The effect is so beautiful that I find tears leaking down my cheeks.

At 9.00 am I turn the sign to 'Open', and unlock the door. People pass by. Some glance through the window, others hurry past, glued to their phones. After nobody has come in by 9.30 am my stomach is churning with anxiety. My parents and Sean are sitting in the back room chatting over coffee, and Shelley is checking each arrangement, turning them a few degrees this way, a few degrees that way, and swapping a yellow flower for a red one.

'Stop worrying Alice,' she says. 'You've only been open half an hour. It's going to be fine. Relax.'

I busy myself sorting out the pots of herbs, making sure they are all labeled correctly. The most popular are rosemary, varieties of mint, thyme, basil, parsley, dill and the love/hate cilantro. Beside them I place a board where people can order any herbs not in stock.

The sudden noise of the phone going off makes me jump.

'Good morning, this is Shelley at Blossoms. Thank you for calling. How may I help you?'

She nods and pulls a notepad towards her. 'Yes, we have beautiful tulips. Which color would you like?' She scribbles on her pad. 'Two dozen yellow tulips, that's fine. Would you like to collect them, or if you prefer we can deliver to you. There's no charge for delivery within town… Yes, they are wrapped in brown paper, tied with string. All grown by us, totally organic and chemical-free. If I may take your address, and your card details please… That's lovely. Thank you so much. As you are our very first customer, we would like to offer you a pot of herbs as a gift. Do you have a favorite?'

She listens intently, smiling and nodding.

'Thank you so much. Enjoy your flowers and have a great day!'

She replaces the receiver with a flourish, and calls out:

'Sean, I have a delivery for you, Alice, may I have a

pot of basil, please.'

She takes a roll of brown paper and a ball of string from under the counter, and expertly wraps the flowers, tying them with string with a small 'Thank you for shopping at Blossoms' card attached.

Sean was very reluctant last week when I said I wanted him to wear a helmet doing the deliveries in town. 'You are too important to the shop and to me, to risk having an accident,' I said. He sulked for an hour, until I gave him a hug and said 'What would I do if anything happened to you? Would you want to make me a widow before we're even married? Come on, Sean, if only to please me.'

He appears from the back room and makes a show of putting on the helmet, rolling his eyes but smiling. Shelley carries out the flowers and hands them to Sean while he mounts his skateboard, and away he shoots, shouting: 'Flower delivery for Blossoms! Flower delivery for Blossoms,' causing people to stop and stare.

'What did I tell you,' laughs Shelley, hugging me. 'We're on our way.'

Shelley was my first friend, and she'll always be the best. We met at college, where being dyslexic she had problems, and with my reputation for being weird, and strange things happening around me, I was isolated. As two outsiders we bonded and have been close friends ever since. She has two cute little girls. Her husband left after the birth of their second child, leaving her to raise them alone and she's known some hard times, but happily she met Sean's friend James at my BBQ last year. He's achingly shy and as gentle as a kitten. They make a perfect match.

It turns out that she was born to be a saleswoman. Not only is she very artistic, but she has an uncanny knack of knowing exactly what a customer would like. Her bubbly personality makes everybody take to her. The only area where she needs my help is writing the plant labels where she sometimes mixes up letters and gets certain words back to front. We giggle every time I ask her if we will need more 'narcations' and 'macellias'.

People start to stop to examine the buckets of flowers outside. Some peer through the window and others venture inside. Most of them are 'just looking', and we leave them to just look, no pressure. Quite a few end up buying something, even if it's a simple pot of parsley.

Back from his delivery, (received 'ecstatically', he reports), Sean wonders whether he should skate around town shouting out that the new shop is open. We gently dissuade him. We're going for the 'hidden little gem' ethos, classy, high quality but not expensive.

A few minutes after 2.00 pm, while Astrid and I sit in the back room making plans for next week, Shelley yells: 'Alice! There's a film crew outside!'

Rex Tillman is standing in the road, waving his arms at his cameraman.

People gather around, and Tillman points to a white

Mercedes coming down the road. A chauffeur hops out and opens the back door.

'Action!' calls Tillman.

Out from the car steps Sita, the glamorous Indian actress who became my friend, despite marrying Jai, the man I once loved.

The crowd grows, people screaming out her name. Sita walks up to me and pulls me into a hug, turning us towards all the flashing cameras. 'Big smile,' she whispers, 'that's what they want to see.' Shelley sweeps open the door to the shop, and Sita looks around. 'Beautiful, Alice. Absolutely perfect.' She takes dozens of photos, including Shelley and me: 'Instagram' she smiles. 'I wish I could stay longer, but I wanted to be here for you today to help you have the best possible start. And I want to wish you happiness, too, with Sean. I am glad for you. I'll be in touch again next time I'm in town.'

She selects a posy of freesias 'My very favorite flower,' she smiles, and insists on paying for them despite my protests. Before leaving she hugs me again and stops outside the shop, holding the freesias to her nose and putting on a rapturous face before she steps into the car and is chauffeured away, waving to the crowds.

Returning from another delivery, Sean rocks his skateboard to a halt when he sees the crowds. The cameraman captures the look of astonishment on his face for the final clip.

26

A different tower

Cory

There follows the most dreadful silence. Decima looks down at me with a bemused half-smile. A drop of rain rolls down her magnificent nose and lands on my chin with a tickle. I try to laugh it off but I'm so nervous it comes out as a choke and then a coughing fit. Nerves nerves nerves eh. Her smile turns to a frown. An 'are you kidding me' frown? Is this a joke frown?

I reach up, grab hold of a crumbling turret and, rather inelegantly, clamber up. I turn to see her arms stretched out, her head tilted to one side, beckoning me forward. We stand entwined. I didn't know that was going to happen any more than she did. Propelled by… love? Yes, of that I'm sure. But also a powerful sense of history and, I suppose, grief. With Jonty freshly gone, I'm as close to my own death as I'm ever going to be and, in this moment, I've never felt more alive. Up here in the wind and rain, it feels like we're flying. Taking her tight, tight hug as a yes, I am the first to speak.

'That must have come as a shock. I'm sorry.'

'I think you're more freaked out than I am.'

'True,' I find a laugh in me from somewhere.

Another long silence. She hasn't said yes yet. This is excruciating.

'So this wasn't planned?'

'No. There's no ring. I'm sorry. Well, there are. Several. In the family vaults. We'll need to take a trip into Lewes.' I tilt her chin up and look into her eyes. 'If you say yes, that is.'

'I've never been wife material, Cory. That's the truth of it.'

'Those crazy times are over, Decima. Josh is dead. Sean, well, Sean…'

She giggles. 'Alice and Sean are as one. But Ramon…'

'How about you have a Ramon pass? If he ever comes back from Korea that is.'

'How about we both have a Ramon pass?'

'Even better.'

We seal the deal with a kiss.

I push back her hood and hold the back of her neck, stroking with my thumb right where she likes it. We gaze across the rolling hills, fading to mist and cloud.

'This is where my father proposed to my mother.'

'Oh?'

'And his father before him to my grandmother.'

'So you did plan it!'

'It was high in my subconscious, clearly, before my

knee took on a mind of its own. I intended to fill you in on my rather sordid family history. As an end to the tour kind of thing. But then, it felt like not only the right thing to do but the only thing to do.'

'Tell me then… tell me what kind of a family I'll be marrying into.'

There it is. The yes! I want to laugh and cry at the same time. The crying wins, it comes out as a choke. I cough it away.

'I'm sorry to be such an old-fashioned twerp, Decima. Can you say it? Can I hear you say it?'

'Let's get out of this weather first, and back to our room. Then I'll show you what a big fat sexy yes feels like.'

Back at the pub, we stay in bed for the rest of the afternoon.

That evening, over The Sportsman's famous vegan sausages, mash and onion gravy, tucked in beside the fire in the snug, I fill Decima in on my family story. She takes it well. I pepper the sadness with some of the jollier times before alcohol got Jonty and bankruptcy and a suicide pact took ma and pa.

We talk about her own family. Her real parents, gone too soon. Her one sibling, like Jonty and I, until death it seems, estranged. We really are two peas in a pod.

The next day, we take a cab into Lewes. Even allowing for the slowness of our legal systems, and the general uselessness of Robertson Siviter, our hopeless family lawyer, he should have been in touch by now.

'Ah Lord Cholmondeley, Sir, my condolences to you,' Robertson greets us with a groveling little bow and damp handshake. His hairline has receded and his forehead grown alarmingly since I last saw him, giving his face a piggy, luminous, sheen. I can tell from his exaggeratedly dipped eyes that it's not going to be good news.

After a few thin smiles and fake pleasantries, as brief as possible because we both know this is all on my dollar, he gives me the news. No. He cannot show me Jonty's Will, or allow me access to jewelry in the family vault.

'And why is that?' I ask rather needlessly.

'You are not the executor, sir.'

A chill rises from the pit of my stomach. It's one thing to suspect something, but when the truth is confirmed it's quite another. 'She didn't marry him, did she? So surely…'

Decima squeezes my hand.

Robertson takes a deep breath and shakes his head, 'She didn't marry him, sir, but he did change his Will. Almost a year ago now.'

'Before his accident, you mean? And you did that for him?'

'I can't discuss other clients, my Lord. Data protection laws and so forth you understand.'

'But he was my *brother.*'

'I've disclosed too much already. Could be struck off. Terribly sorry. Awful shock for you.' He lifts his arm into the air, crooks his elbow and takes an exaggerated look at his watch. A nasty pink digital thing that matches the stripes on his shirt.

We take our leave and go to a tea house to regroup.

I google Wills and fill Decima in on dodgy Robertson who, somewhat like Erica, dipped his paws into my parents' assets a long time ago.

'It's illegal for anybody except the executor to see the Will until probate is granted,' I read out.

'Until everything is hers,' says Decima.

'Then it's public knowledge, anybody can gain access.'

'But what about the jewelry, in the vault, that was your parents' stuff. To be shared between you, surely?'

'Everything is frozen until the wretched probate is granted.'

'What's probate exactly?'

'It's the legal document that gives permission to deal with someone's estate after their death.' I google probate and twins to see if that has bearings on anything. My heart sinks. 'Oh no.'

'What?'

'There are delays at HM Courts and Tribunals. It could take a year. Or more.'

'*What?* But surely Jonty had no right to sign over your half of your parents' inheritance?'

'He was the older brother, Decima. If only by a few minutes. That's how it works in this country.'

'I cannot believe that. The jewelry too?'

'Who knows. Let's try not to think about what hasn't happened yet.' I stand to go. 'Let's turn this day around. I do have an engagement gift for you which you might enjoy more than a ring. For now, in any case.'

The next morning, Decima is lying on the bed with her new phone.

She's ecstatic to be in touch with the world again. Family only, I've ordered. By which I mean Astrid and Alice. Not Pam. We still have to be careful.

The plan is to confront Erica this morning, but before we leave I get a call.

'Ah Lord Cholmondeley… haven't stopped thinking about you since your visit. Thought I'd better fill you in on the legalities old chap. Quite understand it's all come as a bit of a shock for you. So now, listen here.'

Listening any more to Robertson Siviter is the last thing I need right now. But I let him speak.

'*Off* the record…'

I let him speak. When he's finished, I close the conversation as quickly as I can and stare, wide-eyed at Decima.

'What's up? You look like you've seen a ghost.'

'Something like that.'

'What is it?'

I consider going out for a walk, I would rather be on my own right now. I need focus. If I'm going to listen to my gut, Decima might try to dissuade me. But I felt my reaction, as loud and clear as I ever did. I must follow my instincts.

'That was Robertson. There's been a development.'

'What sort of development? Cory, what is it, what's happened?'

'Jonty's will.'

'Yes?'

'It's worthless.'

Decima jumps up, 'How? Why?'

'Entailment.'

'What's that?'

'Entailment is an aristocratic inheritance law. Ancient. Goes back centuries. The castle and the land can never be left to anybody outside the family. Even in a Will. It was a way of keeping estates together. It's still the law today.'

'Why on earth didn't he tell us that yesterday?'

'Over-interpretation of data protection I guess. Or trying to cover his tracks face to face… Planning all along to tell us from a safe distance.'

'He's your family lawyer, he should be on your side! But anyway, that's good news at least.'

'Is it?'

'What do you mean?'

'To be frank, I was glad to be shot of it.'

'Oh?' she pauses to think. 'The castle, yes, I get that.'

'A weight off my back. Let her stay there. If it means so much to her. She's dealt with all of the tedious executor duties already.'

'But how come? If the Will was void?'

'I told you Siviter was useless. For that I'm grateful. It saved me the bother.'

'But all that land. You can sell it? Right? Or are you not allowed to…'

'Yes, I can sell the land. Eventually. When probate is finally granted, but for now… I'm thinking. Well, until then: let her stay.'

Our eyes meet, both minds whirring.

'You'll do anything to avoid conflict, Cory. But I do see what you mean.'

I start breathing again. 'It's no bad thing to have somebody living there in the meantime. She does seem to have truly been fond of Jonty. It's his child after all…'

'Possibly his child.'

'Probably his child.'

'So… do we tell her?'

'Yes. But not officially. We'll keep the lawyers out of it.'

'She might not believe you?'

'That's her problem.'

27

More Jane Eyre than Austen

From: Twinkletoes339@gmail.com
To: AliceAx12@gmail.com

Hey Alice,

It's me! I have my own UK phone at last. I'm not allowed to talk about all that's going on there. I hope you're all OK. I gather that Tillman guy is snooping around big time… There I go, mentioning it already. Delete, delete, delete. Please know I'm thinking about you all the time.

We're fine and well. Trenmaddick Castle isn't what I expected or what you see on google (you must have googled it by now). From a distance, yes, storybook. A big square of thick old bricks on top of a hill with turrets for the bows and arrows and a round Rapunzel tower. It's medieval, Alice. Built in the 11th century! You know what that means? Uninhabitable. And pretty much worthless. His parents tried giving it away to the historical buildings charities. Nobody wanted it. That story has a real sad ending, not for email.

There are arrow slits, big old stone windows and massive fireplaces you can walk inside, timber floors that creak at every step and coats of arms everywhere. The views over the Sussex hills are like something out of Jane Austen. But, you know what, that's about as far as it goes.

Inside it's straight out of a horror film. There are wooden staircases with thick dark wood handrails that change angles every few steps, dried flowers full of dust sticking out of old cracked vases. There are all these creepy old servants' passages (all the people who worked there left long ago) that go down to the dungeons and up to a whole other level of floor you can't get to any other way. There's a snooker table up there, covered in dust, and that's about it. Oh, and that tower. Then there's the actual crazy woman living in the kitchen. More Jane Eyre than Jane Austen then. The place is cursed, Alice. It's evil and I can't wait to come home.

We're staying down at the pub. A real olde worlde pub, Sean would love it. You'd love it. We have a 4-poster bed and there's a dog we take for long walks called Bovril. So it's not all bad.

The main reason I'm writing, Alice, is to say thank you and sorry. I truly appreciate all that you and your family have done for me. I'm feeling guilty at how I treated you and how kind you've been to me.

Cory and I have been getting along really well. We've been united in dealing with the crazy kitchen woman, Jonty's pregnant girlfriend Erica. I keep check on his natural empathy towards her. Though I'm learning about the power of kindness big time. Cory is an amazing person. As are you. In a way, if it wasn't for Sean, you and Cory would be so good together. I'm joking, Cory is mine now, as much as Sean is yours. All that wild sharing and group stuff is firmly in the past. I shudder when I think how I treated you, Alice. 'Being' you has changed me. I truly am a better person.

LATER I've been trying to keep a big secret here but I'm failing big time. Between that last paragraph and this was a large gap of time. Nearly a week. We've been arguing about our News. He's finally agreed we cannot wait until we're home to tell you all.

So here it is: we're engaged. And yes, I'll be Lady Cholmondeley. For all his hatred of possessions, I think Cory really cares about that. The last link to his parents I guess. There are clauses I won't go into here, let's just say I don't think Ramon will mind. Cory's going to message him with the news. Like, simultaneously, so you all know at the same time. Together. Always together.

Decima

28

Beer and crisps in the snug

Cory

We're tucked into our favorite fireside snug, giggling to ourselves. We've just started breathing normally again after Erica's departure. She's been in here a few times over the week. She arrives like Lady Muck, throwing an imperious look around the room before heaving herself up onto Jonty's stool. There, she rules the room. Telling anybody who will listen about her plans to turn *her* castle into a yoga retreat, a cold therapy center or an escape room, depending on the day.

It could be years before probate is granted and she learns the truth. Her pie-in-the-sky dreams will soon fade as the practical realities bite. Decima loves a fight. Keeping the lid on arguments has been tough for her, but, bar a few glacial looks here and there, she's learning. She realizes that it's so much more fun to have our secret. And, more to the point, to leave on good terms. Erica was truly fond of Jonty, that much is clear. And she's promised to keep us posted about the baby. My nephew after all. Life goes on, as they say.

I'm trying to raise Ramon before he hears about our engagement from the others.

'He's not coming through.'

'I've pressed SEND now,' Decima takes a sip of my Guinness. 'The news is out there.'

'No going back now then.' We grin stupidly at each other. She's got white froth from the Guinness on her upper lip.

'He's probably working, what time is it there?'

'Working or whoring, one or the other.' I gently wipe the froth with my little finger.

'Whoring, Ramon? No! He's classier than that.' She rips open the crisps. Bovril, who has been dozing at her feet, leaps to attention. 'Geisha, maybe? I can see him going that route.'

'Geisha is Japan. They have a similar thing in South Korea. Except they're more willing to, well… put it out, he tells me.'

'You two been having naughty boys' talk?'

'He's telling me what's happening, that's all. It's you and I who have changed, remember.'

'He must be having the time of his life, the dirty stopout.'

'Will he ever grow out of it, that's the question. Why are you laughing?'

'Ramon!' she scoffs, handing Bovril a crisp.

I stretch my legs towards the fire, curl my toes and join Bovril in gazing at this miraculous woman at my side.

The light from the flames lifts the gold in her hair. The blond is fading. She looks less like Alice and more the old Decima now. But a new Decima. Softer. Though that fire in her belly, her truth, isn't going anywhere. I'm brought out of my reverie by a sudden thought. If we don't leave soon, she won't match the passport.

Later that evening, my phone beeps. My message has finally reached Ramon.

Hey, what's up?
Ramon! Everything OK there? I got news.

Ramon takes it a bit weirdly. First, he thinks it's a joke. Then he feels betrayed. I reassure him we have discussed visiting rights as soon as he's back home. He doesn't believe me.

'I'm telling you. You were at the proposal, man. Literally right there. We talked about you more than we talked about ourselves. Picture it. Me, on top of that tower with my knee all soggy from going down with the question.'

'You said those words? Will You…. I can't even say it here, now…'

'Oh yes. I did. You will say them too, one day. You will, Ramon. When you know it's right, you'll know.'

'So tell me? What changed? We were always there for each other, like, in the sack, whenever we wanted it? We had the best time, man! All of us. Especially Decima!

How have things changed so much? I'm feeling a little left out here, I'm not gonna lie.'

'Well, you're not. Things got more… emotional. We love you as much as we always have done and always will.'

'That's what I'm sayin? We've always been tight. Tight as can be. So, what changed?'

I sigh. I get what he's saying. I understand his feelings. We really will both be there for him. But how do you explain falling in love?

29

Cock a hoop

Decima

The engines switch from purr to rumble. I fasten my table to the seat in front. Cory fumbles for his eye mask. We bank left, the wing dips and my home city unfolds beneath us, a mosaic of muted grays, browns and blacks. Tiny lozenges dotting the harbor grow into rusty container ships as we descend. England's tapestry of green fields, quaint villages and that cursed ruin of a castle are nothing but a memory.

Towards the horizon the city dissolves into sea mist, the outline of lakes and mountains just visible. That's where Pam's place is. 'Twinkle and Barney, Twinkle and Barney,' I whisper, 'Mummy's coming home.'

But somewhere down there too are Gauld's goons. Ready to hunt me down if my existence is leaked.

Coming in to land, I reach for Digby before jolting upright. Cory grabs my hand.

'I'm so proud of you,' he smiles, gripping hard.

'I can't believe I did that.'

'It was the right thing to do.'

170

'Totally spur of the moment.'

'Gut. Where all the right decisions come from.' He pulls on his eye mask and leans back.

I smile to myself as I remember the confusion on Erica's face. Before she could put him in the bin, or I could snatch him back, Cory had to explain that Digby wasn't a baby toy but a priceless heirloom teddy.

'His name's Digby. He's been through a lot and he came out the other side,' I said. 'And you will too.'

I *am* proud of my gesture, and Cory is *cock a hoop* as he calls it. Cock a hoop! I'm turning into an English Lady already.

'

30

Reunion

Alice

I stay outside and watch the film crew pack up, taking it all in. My breath quickens, I can't believe what I'm seeing. Among the crowd, I spot a familiar figure. He's very tall. He has his arm around the shoulders of a small, round person wearing a shiny purple track suit and a baseball cap. I blink, but when I look again, they've gone.

When the crew drive off, a surge of customers comes towards the shop, phones waving, people shouting. I dash inside to help. Astrid takes over the till whilst Shelley selects and wraps the flowers. I refill the buckets from the back room as they sell out. Patrick has to rush home to collect more freesias as people are fighting over them. To calm them down, I shout that a new delivery is on the way. It's quite a challenge handling such a rush, but we're all good humored and the customers pick up the vibe. We end up dancing around each other singing and laughing.

By closing time, all that remains are a few fallen leaves

and petals to sweep up from the floor. We could not have had a better opening day. We are footsore, hungry, thirsty, sold out, and elated. My father lifts me off my feet and swings me around. 'Alice! I am SO proud of you. This was your idea, your dream, and you have blown me away.'

My mother raises her eyebrows.

The crowds are drifting away. I pull down the blinds on the windows, when somebody taps on the door.

'Sorry, we're closed now,' I call.

'Even to friends?' laughs a familiar voice.

With a shriek I open the door and in steps Cory and his little round companion. She pulls off the baseball cap, extracts a cushion from inside the shiny tracksuit and throws them on the floor.

'How did I ever agree to this?' spits a furious Decima, struggling out of the tracksuit and kicking it away to reveal a powder blue cotton top over skin-tight black leather pants. She stands there glaring angrily at Cory, who is bent over with laughter.

'Ah, the beautiful butterfly emerging from her chrysalis,' says my father, smiling and holding out his arms. 'Come and give me a hug.'

With a wry smile she lets him put his arms around her. 'You old smoothie,' she murmurs.

'I hope you appreciate me doing this for YOU,' she says, turning and pointing at me. 'Risking my life coming to support your little flower shop.'

'I couldn't be more flattered and grateful to you, Decima. It's great to see you both. Thank you so much for making it back on our special day. It means a lot. Now we all want to hear about your adventures in England.'

'Back home now, everybody,' says my mother bossily. 'Time to open a few bottles of my champagne to celebrate. How did you two get here?'

'Subway and walking.'

'Good. Then you must come in the van with us. It's parked out at the back. Nobody will see you, Decima. Better bring your disguise with you though.'

'Right, everybody, let's go,' Patrick calls.

'I have to get back to my girls,' Shelley says. 'James will probably be tearing his hair out by now. See you on Monday, everybody, and thank you all for this fabulous opportunity.'

We've settled ourselves in the van when Sean's phone rings. He smiles, and then frowns. 'Ah, that's my mate Gus. Needs me to go for a quick drink with him.' He looks at me, anxiously.

'Needs must! Off you go then. You know where to find us when you're ready. Go and have fun, you've earned it. Be careful in the dark, now.'

'I won't be that long. Just a quick one.' He gives me a quick peck on the cheek, jumps on his board and skates away.

'Funny,' remarks Decima as we turn off the main road and onto the Brent Flats. 'I feel as if I'm going home.

More than I've ever felt before. Who'd have thought your messy old house could make me feel so safe.'

Cory gives her a sharp jab in the ribs, but Astrid laughs.

When we reach our messy old house, Astrid shoos us all inside. 'Go ahead,' she says. 'I'm going to sow a few freesias for next week.'

'Next week? Surely they take several months to grow,' says Cory.

'Some do, Cory,' she says knowingly.

Zylch is perched on top of the fridge and flies to my shoulder, brushing against Decima on the way and tweaking her hair with a giggle.

She shrugs. 'After what I've been through, nothing can scare me anymore. Not even this thing.' Zylch hops onto her arm and turns his face up to hers, purring. 'It is actually quite cute, whatever it is.'

'I still haven't the faintest clue as to what it is,' says Cory. 'And how it's operated.'

'All done,' Astrid comes back into the kitchen, brushing compost off her hands. 'Now, first of all, let's hear what Cory and Decima have been up to all this time, and as soon as Sean gets back, we'll crack open some champagne.'

We pass round random dishes of food she's excavated from the fridge. Time goes by, sitting relaxed, laughing at Decima's description of Erica and the crumbling property, and I'm so chilled out that I let slip about my narrow escape from delivering drugs. My parents are shocked at first, but laugh when I describe Zylch scaring off the man who came to threaten me. It feels good to be here, together, everybody happy. All we're doing now is waiting for Sean. Where is he? He should be back by now, he's been gone over four hours. I pull out my phone to call him, and see I've missed six calls because I had the phone on 'silent' at the shop and forgot to change it.

I try to ring him back, but there's no reply. 'Call me back when you get this message, Sean. Sorry, my phone's been on silent. Love you.'

Should I be worried? Is he too drunk? Has he had an accident? Is his phone switched off? If he's not here soon, we'll have to go and search for him.

'Folks, it's almost 11.00 pm, I think we'll open a bottle now. There's plenty more for when Sean arrives.'

Astrid wiggles the cork, which flies out of the bottle and bounces off the window frame sounding like a gunshot. Decima shrieks and throws herself to the floor.

Laughing, Cory helps her back onto her feet. 'Come here, you silly goose,' he says. It's noticeable how close they've become and how they've both changed since returning from England. Cory seems less laid back, more assertive, and protective of Decima. She has mellowed, isn't so sarcastic and snappy any more. She smiles now, a genuine smile of pleasure. I think they are a perfect couple and I'm so happy for them.Astrid pours the champagne into a selection of mis-matched glasses and we clink them together.

'Here's to us all, and to Sean,' says my father. 'May we all enjoy long life and happiness.'

If only Sean would hurry up and get here. We're all tired by now and I'm beginning to feel a bit peeved as well as worried. I know what he was like when he used to drink, but I thought he'd changed.

Decima stands up and stretches. 'Cory, it's time we were going. We'll catch up with Sean another time.'

'Yep, milady, at your service.' Cory bows and tugs at an imaginary forelock.

'I'll drive you home,' says my father.

'Oh, um, I forgot we don't have the car here,' Cory says. 'I'm so sorry to have to put you out.'

'It's no problem at all. Now, where are my keys?'

He's patting his pockets and searching the dresser, when Zylch gives a throaty snarl.

'What's the matter with...' I start to say, when suddenly there's the roar of powerful engines outside.

Thinking it's somebody bringing Sean home, my father strides into the hall and pulls open the door. I hear him curse, slam the door and lock it. He runs back into the kitchen and hisses: 'Everybody, be very, very quiet and do exactly as I say.'

We all freeze where we're standing, watching as he swiftly steps to the dresser and taps on the wall next to it. The dresser swings out silently, and he motions us to go behind it.

Cory puts his arm around Decima and sweeps her in. I follow, Astrid comes after me, and my father last of all, tapping the wall again so the dresser closes behind us.

31

Home again

Decima

She's pulled it off. My girl has got this exactly right. Blossoms stands out like a beacon. A riot of color literally exploding out of its corner plot. We could be in Williamsburg here.

'Now remember,' Cory says as we approach the shop, 'keep your head right down until we're safely behind closed doors.'

I flex my hands, pull down my hat and we merge into the crowd. I breathe in the smells of Hawk Bay City, sharp in my senses after the fresh Sussex winds and rain. Dope, diesel and the faintest whiff of rotting vegetables. Home!

Right when we think it's all over, a white car pulls up with a film crew in tow. A beautiful woman emerges in full make-up and glam, ready for the cameras. I recognized her at once. Sita, the cookery book writer. My heart sinks as memories flood back. So much has happened since she came on my show. I touch my cushion padding disguise. I'm a frump. An invisible frump. A nasty invisible frump. The guilt is back with a vengeance. How cruel was I to Alice back then? And how kind have Alice and her family been to me ever since?

Cory senses my mood. 'It's OK,' he whispers, and puts his arm around me. 'It's all OK.' His reassurance works. At least now I can scorn the superficiality of my old life and relish the present moment. Our future together, our admiration for Alice and all that she has created here are the main thing. What we will all become, together is all that matters.

When the crowds finally clear, we step up to the door.

I pull off my disguise and everybody goes nuts. If I feel truly loved by Cory, now I feel truly adored by my family too. Family. It's quite something isn't it. Patrick draws me in for a hug, I make some sarky joke to Alice and she says, with a laugh, that she's glad the real Decima is still in there. I'm only glad I'm me and she is she.

Sean stands at the back of the store. Reticent. Watching me quietly.

We don't talk until we're all leaving the shop.

'Come on, Sean, give me a hug. What do you make of our news? Are you happy for us?'

He squeezes my arm and makes an excuse to leave.

I step back and give him an exaggerated 'Can't it wait?' shrug. To show him I'm offended. He lowers his eyes and turns the other way.

What's so important that he has to go now? We all watch him zap off on his Blossoms branded skateboard.

'Flower delivery for Blossoms! Flower delivery for Blossoms,' he calls merrily. Everybody laughs. He's fine. I was imagining it. If he's peeved at Cory and me, he'll soon get used to it.

Our Sean always was a moody one. He has a special way, a way you can't put your finger on, of letting you know he's in a sulk with you.

32

Conversation overheard

Sean

What a day. Alice was so nervous before the shop opened. She's put her heart and soul into it and there were a few last-minute doubts there. We all tried to calm her down, but she was wound so tight she even snapped at me. That showed how stressed she was. I overheard her telling Astrid that she'd tried her own spell to help her calm down, and it hadn't worked.

Her mood was catching and we were all privately wondering if this shop was going to succeed, being in such a rundown area of town. Would anybody come? Were the locals expecting it to be too expensive, would the better-off folk turn up their noses?

The atmosphere was so tense that when the phone rang we all jumped. Shelley dealt with the call, took the order cool as a cucumber, and I was off on my first delivery. Speeding through town, my heart singing with joy and the love of Alice.

Using my skateboard for deliveries was Alice's

brainwave. It gave me the opportunity to be part of the business, it cost nothing to run, doesn't cause pollution, and it was no problem for me carrying bunches and even bouquets. I wasn't meant to, but a few times as I shot by I couldn't resist singing out: 'Woo hoo! Make way, make way for a Blossom's delivery!' which attracted a lot of attention.

After the unexpected appearance of Sita and the camera crew we were spinning in circles trying to keep up with sales and deliveries. At the end of the day we were physically tired but at the same time buzzing. Then. Then! Cory and Decima turned up out of the blue. Everybody goes ape crazy. Everybody except me. To be honest, I've not adjusted to their news. I can't put my finger on why. Maybe because it's so sudden. Maybe I'd have liked Decima to take me to one side and give me the heads-up. Show some manners. We're ex-lovers after all. Isn't there some protocol involved in that? The argument I was going to have with her unreeled in my mind. Then I thought, maybe there's a song in it? And then I was ticking myself off instead. The way my thoughts go, always the song, the next song, back to the song.

We were packing up, ready to get back to Patrick and Astrid's place to celebrate, and I was climbing into the van beside Alice, when my phone went. Anybody else I wouldn't reply, but Gus is a bit special. When I first arrived in the US knowing nobody, with almost no money and trying to survive by busking, I was sleeping under a bridge when I was attacked one night by a guy trying to steal my guitar. Lucky for me, Gus was passing and flattened the guy, picked me up and took me back to his place. It wasn't much of a place, a deserted building behind a junkyard. He was one of the squatters there, living pretty much hand to mouth. He didn't talk much, but he cleaned up my cuts and bruises, fed me, filled me with cheap whisky and let me sleep on his old couch.

If you ask Gus what he does, you won't learn much. 'A bit of this and a bit of that,' is all he'll say. Sometimes he has money, sometimes he doesn't. His gray hair is as long as his beard, getting on in age but fit as a fiddle. He does this disappearing act for weeks on end. If you ask where he's been, he always says the same thing. 'Here and there.' 'Here and there! Where's here and where's there, Gus,' I banter and we're off on one again.

He's what you might call a free spirit. Does what he wants, when he wants, asks no questions nor answers them. I see him maybe three times a year, he always asks if I'm OK, do I need any help, and to give him a call if so.

When I see his name on my phone, I think right away he must be in trouble, because he's never called me before. So, much as I want to be back home with everybody, I take his call.

It's not what I thought. He'd seen Tillman's report on the shop opening.

'Hey kid! You sure landed on your feet, and what a

catch you've got there. There's a pint waiting for you, so get yourself down here to Murphys.'

Now, I'm truly glad he's not in trouble, but, seeing as I'd rather keep my distance from Decima for a bit longer. I can't say why exactly., I love Alice more than life itself. But feelings are feelings and it's as good a way as any to let her know I'm a tad peeved. Alice doesn't mind and I'll only have the one. So much for that. When I leave, Decima doesn't even notice. I skateboard down to the harbor bar where the port workers hang out. It's a pretty rough place but friendly enough if they know your face.

'You sly pup!' laughs Gus, patting me on the back and nearly knocking me over. 'Look at yourself – scruffy kid makes good. Come over here and tell me how you did it.'

He pulls me over to a booth and raises a pint of Guinness. 'Here's to you, Sean, a happy life and a long one.'

I click my glass against his and gulp the creamy, velvety beer. I haven't eaten a thing since breakfast so the alcohol goes straight to my head. Gus slaps down another glass, and I finish that too. I need to slow down, because since becoming part of Alice's family I no longer drink the way I used to.

As usual Gus will only say he's been here and there, doing this and that. He wants to know everything about me. The job at the Tower, the fire, and most especially how a yokel like me has hooked a girl like Alice.

'How did you know?' I ask.

'Did you not know you were on the television this afternoon?' he says. 'Five o'clock news bulletin, there's that beautiful Indian actress stopping to visit the new shop, and then there's you grinning like a monkey. And there you are in the Herald Online: 'fiancé of Miss Archer.' I could hardly believe what I was seeing, but I'm that happy for you, Sean. You're a lovely lad. Drink up now.'

'Ah, I really shouldn't. I need to be on my way shoon. Alish will be wondering what'sh happened to me.'

'Hee hee, now you're talking like a married man already!'

I feel my face flushing. 'Go on then, jusht one more.'

Chuckling, Gus goes over to the bar and starts chatting with a mate while he's waiting for the order.

Somebody walks quickly past me and stops at the booth behind. 'Guys, listen up. Call from the boss.'

I'm feeling a tad drowsy, the effects of the beer and tiredness and lack of food, so I'm almost nodding off when I hear the word 'Archer'. My ears prick up and I lean back to hear better. 'Brent Flats,' 'tonight'.

Gus comes back and puts another pint in front of me, and a whisky chaser. 'Get that down you, lad, before you go. I know you're chafing at the bit to get back to your girl.'

I gulp down the beer and chaser, and all the time I'm still trying to hear what they're saying behind me, so I'm only listening to Gus with one ear.

'Gauld's raising hell… wants them…' 'exposed the drug facility' 'certain it's the daughter that was meant to be dead' 'big nose' 'nothing left standing'.

'I think I've lost your attention!' Gus laughs quietly.

'Yeah, shorry. I've had it, better be on my way. Thanksh.'

'Okay, keep being well Sean.' He raises his glass to me and I squeeze his shoulder.

'And yourshelf, Gush. And yourshelf now.'

I get up from the booth and pull out my phone, standing with my back to the people behind, and pretending I'm taking a call. But what I'm really doing is listening to them.

'Joe, call up Greg and tell him to get his boys to meet with us at the old Dupont house on the Flats. Gauld says we'll be going in hard at the Archers, no questions, if it moves, shoot it.'

They all stand up. In a flash, I'm stone cold sober. My heart in my mouth, I stroll to the door, grab my skateboard and race round to the back of the building. I get there in time to see the men climb into their vehicles and pull away.

I ring Alice, but there's no reply. I ring again.
Nothing.

My phone battery is down to 2%. The third time I call she still doesn't pick up. My heart starts racing, my belly clenches, sweat pops on my face. I kick my skateboard into action and head through town, faster than I've ever moved before, heading to the Brent Flats. I try again to call Alice, still no reply. When I reach the Flats I rattle along the bumpy track, faster and faster, gasping and panting. Why isn't Alice picking up her phone? Has something happened before I can get there? Am I too late? My board hits a bump and I fly off, landing on my face and elbow. I pick myself up, grab the board, and see one of the wheels has broken off. I wipe the blood out of my eyes and start running, ignoring the pain in my shoulder, running, running, stumbling and running, running to warn Alice and her family.

I hear car engines behind me, and dodge into the bushes, pushing my way through, brushing away whiplike branches, stumbling on roots. The cars pass me, and I get back onto the path. Past the deserted Harding house, it's another half mile to the old Dupont place, and then another quarter mile to the Archers. I don't know if I can keep going, but I must. I dare not stop calling Alice. I can't risk any delay, so I keep running, every muscle in my body screaming, my heart pounding in my chest, my lungs bursting.

As I near the Duponts I see a group of vehicles parked, and hear voices calling and shouting. In the headlights I see perhaps twenty men, all holding rifles.

I skirt around through the bushes again and put all my energy into getting to the Archer house to warn them. I can see the lights on there now, and I begin shouting.

'ALICE! ALICE! ALICE!' My throat is dry and raw,

but I'm close now. She must hear me any minute.

I hear the engines behind starting up again, headlights light up the track ahead of me, and something punches me in the back. I feel myself falling, falling, falling into darkness and with my last remnant of breath I scream 'ALICE!' but it only comes out as a gasp.

33

Life and death

Alice

I'm shaking and panting, wanting to scream, jammed in this dark, crowded space. I can't breathe, I'm clawing at my throat. I'm so panicked I've forgotten the calming spell.

'It's all right, Alice. It's all right. Just breathe.' My father has wrapped me in his arms and is holding me against his chest.

'Breathe. There's plenty of fresh air in here, coming through that vent up there.' He points to the ceiling.

My heartbeat slows down and the spell comes back to me.

'What on earth What's happening?' Decima shouts.

'Shh. Keep your voice down. We are safe in here from whatever is going on out there. I thought it was someone bringing Sean back, but there are several vehicles lined up facing the house, with powerful lights on. I don't know what it's about, but it's not good. We had some trouble last year, so I created this safe space in case it ever happened again.'

'So that's what you were doing when the kitchen was in a mess!' I say.

'Exactly. Let me find the light switch.'

A second later the space lights up with a soft yellow glow, showing a shelf with bottles of water, packets of cookies and a phone charging point. Now we can see, we spread out a little from the huddle we were in. There's just enough room for the five of us to stand comfortably.

'Guns,' says Decima. 'Where are your guns?'

'We don't have guns. We don't need them.'

'Then what are we meant to do if these people attack us – throw cookies at them?' snaps Decima.

'Have faith, princess. Trust me, we have everything we need to keep us safe. They cannot find us here.'

'Huh,' she grunts, but she calms down. My father has a special way of handling Decima, and I smile to myself.

He slides open a small panel in the wall. It gives a view into the kitchen, through a row of glass tumblers that disguise the opening.

Cory, who hasn't said a word since we entered the safe room, looks around and says: 'A year ago I had a normal life; nothing much happened. Look at me now. I've somehow traveled through space. I have a title, own a shabby castle, have a stunningly beautiful fiancée, and here we are, locked in a cupboard in a house in the middle of nowhere with a couple of witches, expecting to be attacked at any moment by unknown forces. How much weirder can things get?'

He looks so bewildered that I can't help giggling.

Then I remember that we don't know where Sean is, and I am praying that he's safe somewhere.

There's a tremendous crash nearby.

'That's the front door. They've broken in,' says my father calmly.

Decima whimpers. Cory puts his arm around her and a finger to her lips. 'You're safe, sweetheart. Be my lovely brave girl.'

We hear the sound of marching feet in the hall, and the kitchen door swings open.

A voice says: 'They're here somewhere. Look at all these dishes and glasses still full. Art, Mitch, Bobby, Lance, search everywhere upstairs. You three, get into that room on the other side of the hall.'

'Good luck with that,' whispers my mother.

'We now know there are at least eight of them,' murmurs my father.

From above we hear furniture being moved, shouts, running footsteps, curses.

'Mick – they're not upstairs. We've turned it upside down. Defo nobody there.'

'Just a mo - there are five table settings. Who's the extra guest? There's the mother and father, the girl and boyfriend. Must be somebody else here.'

'Can't get into that room across the hall. Feels like the door's made of steel.'

'They have to be somewhere – the van's outside. Have you checked the garage?'

'The boys have been all round, can't find anything.'

'Keep searching. When the boss gets here, I don't want to have to tell him we screwed up.'

'Sounds like we're too late.'

'I 'ope you bunch of idiot clowns 'ave found her,' bellows a most unAmerican voice.

'We've almost found them, boss. Give us a few more minutes to dig 'em out.'

'Dig them out of where, exactly?'

'Pretty certain they're holed up behind that door in the hallway. Seems to be reinforced steel. We're gonna need machinery to cut through it.'

'And I suppose, with you being mastermind, you thought to bring machinery with you?'

'Well, we didn't know that…'

'You didn't know. You didn't know. That's the trouble with you, you never know. I pay you to know, and you don't know. Useless. Totally ****ing useless.'

Decima gasps. 'Gauld!'

My father looks through the spy panel. 'Yes, you're right. I thought it might be. He's the one who caused us trouble last year when he tried to buy us out. What's bought him here now, I wonder?'

'FIND THEM NOW YOU DOZY BUFFOONS,' Gauld bawls, followed by the sound of clattering as he sweeps everything off the table. 'THEY ARE GOING

TO PAY! NOBODY MESSES WITH CLIFF GAULD AND GETS AWAY WITH IT. THEY WRECKED MY PLANS FOR THE LEISURE CENTER, AND NOW THAT STUPID GIRL HAS GOT THE DRUG OPERATION SHUT DOWN. THIS FAMILY ARE FINISHED! DO YOU UNDERSTAND? FINISHED, KAPUT. DONE. EXTINCT.'

'Bobby, get back to the site and find the welding torch. We're going to have to cut through that steel door.'

'Hang on a min,' says another voice. 'Is there a cellar in here?'

'Nah, there wouldn't be. None of these old places out here have cellars.'

'WILL YOU FOOLS STOP TALKING. I DON'T WANT TO BE HERE ALL NIGHT. THERE'S ONE WAY TO GET THEM OUT OR TAKE THEM DOWN. WE BURN THE PLACE.'

Decima shivers but my father just grins. He gives a jaunty little whistle and turns a switch in the wall.

A grinding noise comes from the kitchen, as the table slides to one side, revealing a hatch in the floor.

'SO NONE OF THESE PLACES HAVE CELLARS. IS THAT RIGHT, IDIOT? WHAT DO YOU THINK MAY BE DOWN THERE? PERHAPS WHAT WE'RE LOOKING FOR? GET IT OPEN.'

'As you wish,' my father says quietly, turning another switch.

I peer through the spy panel. The men stand in silence,

watching the hatch rise.

'Here we go! Here we go.' Scenting victory, Gauld has calmed down. 'All of you get yourselves down there and bring them up.'

One by one the men climb down, and with a sigh of satisfaction Gauld flops down onto a chair and lights up a cigar. He puts his feet in their pointy cowboy boots up on another chair and picks up a piece of cheese from the floor. He rubs it on his trousers and pops it in his mouth.

In the safe room, my father asks my mother if he should go ahead. She nods. He fiddles with a couple of switches. The hatch to the basement slides half closed as screams and shrieks of terror fill the air.

Gauld jumps off the chair and pulls a pair of pistols from holsters around his waist. An ashen face appears through the narrow gap in the hatch as its owner scrabbles to haul himself out. The screaming gets louder, with shouts of 'HURRY UP'.

Gauld stands over the hatch, scowling. He's knocked off his feet by a tangle of arms and legs as the frantic men scramble to escape.

'What the **** is going on?' he bellows, snatching at the legs of one of the fleeing men who wrenches himself free, kicking him on the nose.

All eight men run blindly through the kitchen, knocking into furniture and each other, out into the hall and through the front door. As the last one dashes through the door he turns and shouts, 'Monsters!

Monsters! There's a dungeon full of monsters down there!' Engines start up and roar loudly away, leaving Gauld shouting in vain for them to stop.

He returns to the hatch and hesitates.

'Go on,' hisses my mother. 'Why don't you go down there, you evil creature.'

But he steps back, dabs at his bleeding nose and scratches his head, staring round the room. He begins tapping on the walls with his guns, trying to detect a hollow.

'I think it's time for us to have a little chat with Mr Gauld,' says my father. 'Are we all in agreement?' We all nod. He pushes a button and the panel slides quietly open.

As he steps out into the kitchen, Gauld spins round.

'Are you looking for something?' asks my father politely.

Gauld's eyes bulge with shock.

'Where did you come from?'

'I could ask you the same thing. What are you doing in my house?'

'I've come to settle some debts, that's what I'm doing. Your refusal to sell ruined my plans, then your interfering daughter destroyed my business. Your family has ruined me. I've lost everything, even my plane.'

'And you thought bringing a gang of thugs here, to my home, would somehow help?'

'You owe me! Nobody messes with Cliff Gauld. Tell

me where your daughter is and I'll walk away.'

'Fair enough, but first I think there's somebody who'd like to meet you.'

Cory walks out from behind the dresser, holding Decima by the hand.

'YOU! No, that's not right. You're meant to be dead. You should be dead.'

'Thank you so much. I'm glad to see you too,' snarls Decima. 'I hope my survival hasn't inconvenienced you.'

'You were meant to be *dead!*' he roars.

'I'll take that as confirmation and a confession that you were behind the fire at the Tower. Isn't it strange that my parents died in a fire, putting their fortune into your grubby hands, and then I was 'meant' to die in a fire which would put millions of insurance money into your grubby hands too. You disgust me, you vile, greedy monster.'

This is when I step out from behind the dresser, and Gauld loses it.

'YOU! Do you know what you did with your meddling? Because of you I lost my only remaining income. Between your family and that ungrateful brat, I can't keep up repayments of my loan from the Cosa Nostra. Do you know what that means? What they will do to me, now I don't even have the plane to get away?'

Cory has been listening silently, and now he says: 'What a perfectly despicable individual you are. I think you should leave now. You are not the kind of person we wish to associate with.'

'You poncy tosser,' Gauld spits, trembling with rage and raising his guns.

'We are unarmed,' says my father quietly. 'I trust you don't want to add murder to your other crimes?'

'What do I have left to lose except for the pleasure of wiping out the whole stinking lot of you.' He swings from left to right, trying to decide where to aim, when Cory hurls himself at Gauld, knocking the guns from his hands and kicking them out of reach.

'Well done Cory!' Decima crows. 'Now show us how brave you are, you loathsome bag of wind. Five of us, one of you. Not so brave now, are you?'

'What do we do with him now?' asks Cory.

'Kill him!' yells Decima.

'We hand him over to the police,' says my father. 'He's wanted for the drug business, let alone how many other offenses.'

Gauld smirks. 'Ha ha! When you have friends like mine, in high places, you don't have to worry. I have powerful people in my pocket, so do your worst.'

He's distracted by an odd sound from behind. He half turns, then screams as Zylch, who has been perched above the door the whole time, swoops towards him howling, showing a mouthful of fangs and striking out at him with razor sharp claws, drawing lines of blood down his face.

Gauld tries to push him off but Zylch clings on and

bites off his right ear.

Decima laughs and claps her hands.

'Stop!' I yell, fearing what Zylch might do. As evil as Gauld is, we cannot kill him. Our family are not murderers.

Zylch settles down on the floor in front of us, staring at Gauld as he touches his face and examines the blood on his hands.

As if we are all in a photograph, none of us move, Nobody makes a sound.

Gauld grunts and puts his hand to his throat. His eyes roll up into his head, his knees buckle and he sinks in a heap to the floor. Cory strides over and kneels beside him, listening intently and then puts his hand on Gauld's neck, feeling for a pulse.

'He's gone,' he says calmly. 'I imagine his heart stopped when that um, creature attacked him.'

'Good,' cries Decima. 'Perfect solution. But what are we going to do with the body?'

'Leave that to me,' says my mother. 'Patrick, give me a hand.'

They drag the body to the hatch and let it go. It lands with a plopping sound, and my mother climbs down the ladder after it. 'I won't be long,' she calls.'

'I'm going to look for Sean,' I say. 'I don't understand why he hasn't arrived.'

'We're coming with you,' Decima says.

It's dark outside. I use my phone torch to search the

path, calling out Sean's name constantly, but there's no reply.

Cory and Decima are looking nearby. Cory shouts: 'I think I heard something!'

My heart races and I start to run. Two hundred yards from the house a sliver of moonlight breaks through the clouds, and my torch shines on the shattered glass of a phone. I pick it up and see that it's Sean's beloved Samsung Z flip phone.

'Sean!' I call loudly. 'Where are you?'

Nothing.

I keep walking along and around the path, calling his name.

My torch picks up something glinting in the bushes – his silver chain and crucifix.

Pushing through the bushes I run towards it and crouch down. Sean lies there, on his back, silent, motionless, his eyes closed. His face is very white.

'Sean!' I scream. 'Sean!'

He's very still.

'HELP!' I shout. 'HELP! I've found him. Over here.' I flash my phone torch to signal where I am.

I bend down to his face. 'Can you hear me?' I whisper.

No reply.

I place my arm beneath his neck and gently lift his head. One eye half opens. My arm feels wet and sticky.

'Sean, look at me. Open your eyes.'

There is no response.

I hear running feet. I hold his head against my chest and stroke his hair, my tears dripping onto his pale skin. I remember how they once brought Zylch back to life, and cry as hard as I can, hoping against hope they will do the same for Sean.

When my mother reaches us, she kneels beside him.

She feels his pulse and lifts his eyelids, then peels back his shirt and gasps.

She looks up at me and slowly shakes her head.

'But you can do something,' I whisper. 'Surely you can do *something*.'

She stands up and runs back to the house, returning a few seconds later with a tiny flask.

'Lift him up and hold him close,' she says quietly, looking into my eyes.

I fold him tenderly in my arms and hold his head in the crook of my arm, gazing through my tears into his sightless eyes.

Astrid takes the cork from the flask and raises it to his lips, whispering under her breath. I only catch the word '*Serene*'.

Sean stirs in my arms and opens his blue eyes. My heart sings.

'Oh Sean,' I sob.

'Alice,' he says, 'hold me.'

'I love you Sean,' I say, and at that moment it is true. I really do love him. 'I'm holding you. I'm here.'

A shaky hand slowly reaches up and touches my face.

I place my hand over his.

'I'm going to the stars now, Alice, back to the stars. I will wait there for you. I am so happy.'

Through my tears I look into his eyes, then I lean forward and kiss him on his lips. He lets out a small sigh and his face lights up with a smile. I watch as the life leaves him, and a beam of starlight flies away into the night, up, up, up, leaving a trail of tiny stars behind.

Wailing, I brush my tears off his face and rock his body back and forward as it grows colder.

How long do I sit there, numb with misery? I feel Zylch's soft coat brush against my arm and become aware of people around me. A hand reaches around my shoulders.

'He loved you very much, Alice. I never saw him as happy as he was these last months. Look at his face — pure joy, and peace. His last moments were everything he would have wanted.' Decima is kneeling beside me. 'Let the guys take him inside now, and come with me, you're freezing.'

I let her help me to my feet and lead me to the house. Astrid has swept the debris from the kitchen table And lit two white candles.

My father and Cory bring Sean and lay him very carefully on the table. Astrid covers his battered body with a cloth and I place a cushion beneath his head. He looks so innocent, so young, so pale, and yet so peaceful and happy. I cannot stop weeping.

We all stand around the table, heads bowed. We link hands, and nobody speaks for many minutes. Then Cory starts to hum *She's the One*. We each join in, softly. Some notes are replaced with sobs. There are no dry eyes as we pay tribute to Sean, the man we all loved.

34

Aftershock

Alice

By the time the police arrive it is almost dawn.

Waiting for them, we had talked through the events and agreed that we would state, truthfully, that we had been attacked by a gang of men led by Cliff Gauld. We believed that it was a fresh attempt by Gauld to drive my parents away from Brent Flats. Something had startled them and they had fled. Gauld's car is still outside, and we can only think that he had left with some of the others, leaving his car behind. We had not seen or heard anything more of him and know we never will. My mother has taken care of that.

We tell the police how we had found Sean's body, fatally wounded by gunshot. Murdered. It looked as if he had somehow learned of the attack and had tried to get here to warn us.

While we are giving our statements to the police, the forensics team collects evidence from the smashed front door, fingerprints and footprints, fibers and hairs from all over the house. They find no indication of the safe room, nor the hatch to the cellar. Outside they pick up more footprints, tire tracks, cigarette ends and the broken skateboard. They are certain it won't take long to catch the men and find the murderers. I howl when Sean is zipped into a body bag and taken away. There will have to be an autopsy and I cannot bear the thought.

We are all exhausted, but too shocked to sleep. Cory sits staring into space. Decima keeps dabbing tears from her face. We sit in silence while my mother feeds us cinnamon toast and hot chocolate. Eventually, my father drives Cory and Decima home.

My mother puts her arms around me and tells me to go up to bed. She offers me a potion to help me sleep, but I want to be alone. I take Zylch home and lie down on my bed, still wearing my clothes stained with Sean's blood.

He once said he would die for me, and now he has died because of me. My carelessness has caused his death. I was so busy celebrating the success of my shop, I forgot to turn on my phone. When I realized he was late, I should have gone and looked for him, but I didn't. I could have saved his life if I'd been more thoughtful. Now, for the first time I have learned that all the magic in the world cannot bring back somebody from the dead. For all my powers, that is beyond me. I brought Zylch back to life, but Zylch is of the other world, and Sean was human.

Did I really show Sean enough love? Did I make him

feel loved? Did I deserve his love? These are questions that will always haunt me. Somehow, I am going to find a way to make it up to him, so that he will know, up there among the stars, how much he meant to me.

I can't lie here moping all day. We have to get all the plants ready for opening time tomorrow. I shower and spend a couple of hours potting fresh herb seedlings so they will be at their best next week, then I **Brmstick** to my parents.

We pack the van in the evening, selecting all the sweetest smelling and most vibrantly colorful flowers.

The first thing I do when I get to the shop is to place a framed photo of Sean on the wall behind the counter. Inscribed: 'Sean Fahey, musician and very special man, you will be missed forever. Sweet dreams.'

He wouldn't have liked the goofy face photo I picked but I don't want to be maudlin. And, besides, it's my favorite. His curly red hair sticks up around his head like a halo, his blue eyes sparkle with mischief, his tongue sticks out, and the freckles around his nose look like tiny copper coins. I only have to look at it to smile. This is how I want everybody to remember him. Underneath I fix the Blossoms flag from his skateboard.

Even before we open, there are queues on the street. Because of Sita's Instagrams, we've become famous overnight. At any other time we would be wildly excited, and although we all keep our smiles on, our hearts are heavy. The news of the attack and Sean's death have brought the curious, and those who knew and loved him. They offer condolences, share their memories and buy flowers for him. In an hour the shop is empty and the sidewalk covered in layer upon layer of floral tributes. My phone goes all day with messages from friends. Ramon phones from Korea. He's in shock, stumbling over his words and sobbing over the loss of his friend.

We restock the shop twice. By closing time we're all so tired we're barely able to speak. Shelley's partner James was Sean's best friend. When he comes to collect her his eyes are reddened from weeping so much.

'Why? Why would anybody want to hurt the kindest guy you could ever meet? He stepped over ants, he'd give his last cent to anybody who needed it. His life had turned around, he was head over heels in love, he'd found a whole family. I'd never seen him so happy.'

Zylch is waiting when my parents drop me off at home. He's dejected, his ears flattened against his bowed head. He holds his arms/wings up, asking to be held. I pull him to my chest, rest my head on his and stroke his silver fur. We sit in the kitchen and peck at Parmesan cheese, while I make a list of all that needs to be done for Sean, not least find his relatives in Ireland and tell them the news. For that, I need to go to my parents' house and into Sean's cozy little room in the garden shed.

It's immaculately tidy, with a lingering scent of his aftershave, his clothes neatly folded on a bench, his shoes lined up beneath. His guitar leans against the wall. I pick it up and hold it for a few moments, stroke a few strings and then place it carefully back. I find the old leather suitcase where he kept his few possessions and papers.

There's a pile of envelopes with Irish stamps, a photograph album, his passport and identity papers, a phone charger, bible, hymn book, a couple of diaries and a thick notebook in his spiky handwriting containing the lyrics of all his songs. Tucked into a pocket are four memory sticks. I put everything into my backpack to **Brmstick** home. As I leave, I notice the sheriff's car parked outside the house.

Back home, I put his diaries to one side. I won't be reading them. His private thoughts should remain private. I go through the photo album. There's a skinny Sean standing between two old people outside a tumbledown house. Sean in school uniform, one sock up to his knee, the other wrinkled around his ankle. Laughing with a group of boys, jumping off a roof, standing on a beach flexing his arm muscles, holding a skateboard, pulling down his pants to show off his backside, always with that goofy grin of his. Then there are photos of me, dozens and dozens. Working at the Tower, walking in the park, going into my apartment block, coming out, oh my goodness! I had no idea he had all these. There are a couple that are strange. In one I am holding something in my arms, and in another I am bending down to stroke something, but in both photos there's nothing there. Zylch! The camera is clearly unable to capture creatures of the *autremonde*.

I'm about to go to bed when my mother phones to say the men suspected of causing Sean's death and the burglary have been arrested. Partly based on the forensic evidence and partly from talking to Gus, the friend Sean was drinking with. Gus is very much in touch with the lower elements of society in town, and Sean was popular everywhere.

I take the photo of Sean on the beach, kiss it and put it into a frame on my bedside table. Zylch sits at the end of the bed, humming and counting his fingers. My mind whirls briefly, thinking of all that lies ahead, before I fall into a mercifully dreamless sleep.

35

Waking

Alice

What a strange experience, flying in a commercial airline. You don't have any control at all. You are in the hands of strangers. Somebody you don't know is flying the plane, and you're sitting next to strangers in a small chair. I'm finding it quite stressful, locked in here for more than six hours. You can't open a door or window, or get off, come to that, if you want to. Ugh. Not for me, thank you. I prefer my **Brmstick** method.

However, **Brmsticking** with Sean's casket is a step too far, so here I am, locked in this metal tube, taking him to his home in Ireland. First stop, Shannon airport. The **Calm** spell has helped.

My father has dealt with everything. He found Sean's relatives in Killarney, got my photo returned to my passport and handled all the practical arrangements with funeral directors, airlines and paperwork. I am officially in awe of my father. He had so much foresight to plan so well in case of attack. Thank goodness he took the threats from Gauld so seriously. And then how hard and carefully he used his engineering skills to make sure we'd be safe. How bravely and calmly he had faced Gauld. How caring he has been to Decima, and how he has whole-heartedly supported the flower shop. When I have most needed his help, he has done everything for me.

He found me in tears one evening while I was loading plants into the van. 'Ah Alice,' he sighed.

'I'm so confused, I don't know what to do about Sean, whether there should be a service, and how to get him home to his family. It's all too much. I want to do it right for him.'

He said: 'Leave it to me. You concentrate on your shop and let me handle everything else.'

As well as all that he's also doing deliveries for the shop, on a bike.

I've realized that behind his British reserve, he loves me very much and he's showing it now that I need his help. His way of demonstrating his love is to do everything possible to care for me. He's my hero.

Whenever I've struggled, Shelley and my mother have held everything together. We've become busier and busier, by closing time each day the shop is always empty.

I glance at my watch and see we've only been flying for an hour. It seems forever, and I wriggle, wishing I could get up and move around and feel the fresh air on my skin. I miss my shop. I miss Zylch. He's staying with my parents while I'm away.

Yesterday, we held a service for Sean in the Catholic

church of Saint Gregory. That's where he and Ramon used to attend Sunday mass. The church was overflowing, with people even standing outside, down the steps to the street. We had asked the priest to make the service upbeat, which he did, and my father read a loving and sometimes funny eulogy. It's exactly what Sean would have wanted.

Now he's resting in the hold of the plane and I'm sitting here watching my neighbor's white knuckles gripping the armrest as the aircraft bumps up and down over the Atlantic. After I cast a little *Calm* spell to help her she gives a small sigh and closes her eyes. Her hands relax as she falls asleep. I've stuck to my promise to do a small act of kindness every day.

After what seems like forever, a flight attendant makes an announcement in what sounds like a foreign language. I tap my neighbor and ask what the attendant had said. She replies in the same language, and then seeing my blank look says slowly 'We are landing. The plane is coming down to the ground.' She makes a slow swooping motion with her right hand, onto the back of her left hand, then reaches over and slots my seatbelt in. Again, she says something I can't understand, but it's accompanied by a big smile so I smile back. At last the plane glides down, bounces and then rolls to a stop, I pull my backpack down from the locker and follow the passengers into the terminal.

Going through Customs & Immigration formalities, I

think how much simpler my own form of travel is. Whilst I'm standing around wondering what next, the officer examining my passport presses a buzzer and murmurs a few words. A couple of minutes later a friendly man introduces himself, shakes my hand and takes me to a small but quite chi chi lounge to wait for the next step of our journey. The funeral director will collect the casket then pick me up for the drive to Killarney.

I sit quietly with a coffee and pastry listening to the voices around me. Gradually I'm able to tune into their accent and understand what they're saying. It's one of my lucky talents, being able to pick up foreign languages instantly. If the language here isn't actually foreign, it might as well be, with the Irish accent being so strong. Sean sometimes used to put on an exaggerated accent, so that helps too.

'Miss Archer,' calls a soft voice, making me lift my groggy head from the table. 'I'm sorry to wake you, but your transport is here.' I've been asleep for almost an hour.

The officer escorts me to a red estate car, not the black hearse I'd imagined. He introduces me to his cousin, Finn Brady. 'Finn will take you and your man home,' he says, easing me into the passenger seat of the car. Sean's casket is strapped down in the back. There's a green rubber leprechaun swinging from the rear view mirror. I see the officer slip Finn a wad of rolled up bank notes 'for his trouble'.

Finn says it won't take long to get to Molly and Joe's house, which is where I will be staying. Every time the car swerves around one of the many bends in the road, the leprechaun's legs leap up, making it look like it's doing a happy dance. Sean would have loved that. Finn chats about him, one of his many cousins, all the way. We're out in the countryside in no time. There aren't that many pedestrians out here, but the few that there are all stop and bow in respect as we pass. Some cross themselves, one young guy, a farmer I guess, even took his flat cap off and held it to his chest.

Finn seems to know a lot about me and my family. It all sounds good. I grab the door handle as we career around an extra-sharp bend. Finn taps my knee and tells me not to worry. I'm stifling a giggle at the leprechaun which took on a life of its own at that one.

We pull up at a low, whitewashed farmhouse. Finn hoots, and a hefty man comes over and looks in the back of the car. 'Welcome home, Sean, welcome home lovely boy, and bless you.' He wipes his eyes with a handkerchief, then pulls open the driver's door and shakes hands with Finn.

'And this will be our lovely Alice,' he smiles, coming round the car and helping me out. 'Come on out now and let us get a dram inside of you.'

As he leads me towards the house Finn pulls away in the car.

'Sean!' I scream. 'He's taken Sean!'

'Don't be troubling yourself, Alice. Everything has been taken care of, and you've nothing to do. Sean will be fine. Now come on inside and let Molly take care of you. We've a big day tomorrow.'

Molly is a beautiful, softly-spoken, woman who sits me in an armchair by a fire in the lounge and places a tray on my lap. 'There now, you refresh yourself while I leave you in peace and run you a warm bath. After that, we'll get to know each other a little better.'

What a feast. Fluffy bread, still warm from the oven, a dish of creamy butter, a great slab of cheese, a bowl of stewed apples with a jug of cream on the side and a teacup of very strong tea. As I eat, I enjoy the warm glow of the fire, taking in the spacious, low-ceilinged room with its comfortable mis-matched furniture and colorful rugs.

I've finished eating when Molly comes back and finds me with my eyes closed, almost asleep again. She sits beside me. When she's sure I've had enough to eat. Am I sure? Am I sure sure? She explains what will be happening tomorrow. She squeezes my hand and thanks me for bringing Sean home.

'Come, let me show you to your room.' I follow her up a narrow stairway into a small, pretty room with a window looking out onto green hills.

'This was Sean's room when he was a little lad, when the farm belonged to his grandparents.'

From my backpack I pull out Sean's album, and point

to the photo of him standing between two elderly people in front of a tumbledown farm house and hand it to Molly.

'That's him, cheeky imp,' she smiles and nods to herself. 'Could I borrow this for tomorrow? There's many who'd love to see it.'

She gives a sudden sharp intake of breath, her eyes fill with tears but she manages to catch them back with a big choke before they fall.

'It's yours. I have removed the photos of myself and put them with him in the casket with his diaries.'

'That's a beautiful thing you've done, Alice. It's little wonder he loved you so much. He told us you had bewitched him. Would you take a wee nip after your bath to help you sleep? No doubt your clock will be upside down with the time difference.'

What's a wee nip? I've no idea but it sounds like a good idea to help me sleep. She's right about my internal clock. Here it's already 10.00 pm but it's only 5.00 pm at home, and it feels too early for bed. So I thank her and say I'd like that. When I've bathed there's a tray on the bedside table with a slice of fruit cake, a small glass of amber liquid, which I understand is the 'wee nip', and a handwritten note: 'Sleep well and sweet dreams, Alice. I'll give you a call in the morning when it's time for breakfast.'

I sit on the bed, nibble the cake and sip the 'wee nip' cautiously. At first it makes me cough until I dip the cake into it, which helps it go down. I take out my clothes for tomorrow and hang them over a chair, then lie in bed staring at the ceiling and imagining the little Sean here. It's high summer now, but I think of how cold and bleak it would have been during the winter, when he had to get up so early every morning to help his grandparents with their farm before going to school. I wish he could see the old house now, modernized and homely. I wish he was here.

A knock on the door wakes me. 'Breakfast is ready when you are,' calls Molly.

The wee nip clearly did its job. I slept through the night like a baby.

Sean's funeral service is in the local church, which is actually a cathedral, an imposing tall stone building magnificently decorated inside. We arrive early. I feel a lump in my throat when I see the casket in front of the altar, smothered in white flowers. There are only a dozen people there besides ourselves, standing in small groups and talking quietly.

Joe guides us to the front pew. 'Perhaps I should sit a little further back,' I say, 'so that Sean's family can be closer.'

He steers me to the bench. 'Alice, you sit with us. You are family. You will always be part of our family.'

More people enter the church and shuffle into their seats. A few mournful notes ring out from the organ.

'Have you been to a Catholic mass before?' asks

Molly.

'We had a service for Sean in Hawk Bay City. That's the only time I've been in a Catholic church.'

'You've a treat coming today then – we've a Requiem Mass for Sean. It's very special.'

A thought strikes me. 'Was it here that Sean was in the choir? Where Father Ronan encouraged him to learn music? I remember him telling me.'

'Yes, that's right. You'll meet Father Ronan later.'

The organ music begins playing quietly, as the church fills until there's no room left; people are standing in the aisles and outside the door.

'Are all these people Sean's friends?'

She does this odd double intake of breath. She does that a lot. 'Friends, and family.'

There's a hush as the priest, regal in purple robes, arrives at the altar.

It's the most poignant hour I've spent during my life, listening to the Latin service and the beautiful voices of the choir. There's a feeling of serenity, peace, and dignity. It is both very sad, and truly uplifting.

I sit remembering Sean, all the good times we enjoyed together, our trip to the stars, his sense of humor, his kindness, and I see him again setting off from the shop on his skateboard to make our very first delivery.

Sometimes I'm smiling at the memories, and sometimes tears leak down my cheeks.

Once the mass has ended Sean's casket is removed to

be taken to the burial ground. I walk out of the church between Joe and Molly who each have an arm around my shoulder. I'm overwhelmed by all the kind-eyed strangers who come to offer their condolences.

We gather around the graveside in soft sunshine and a warm breeze. A stooped, gray-haired priest recites prayers in a quavering voice. When the casket is lowered into the ground, Molly hands me a red rose that I drop in with a handful of soil. I think I'm expected to weep, but I can't, because Sean isn't down there. He's up in the stars, where we once traveled together.

Walking back to the car we stop to speak to the priest. 'Through Sean's letters we all feel we know you, Alice,' he says, taking my hand in his. 'You are every bit as lovely as he said.'

'You're Father Ronan, aren't you? Sean spoke of you often as the person who saved him from himself. I'm so very happy to meet you.'

'Be assured that he is now at peace in the Kingdom of the Lord and know that he had enjoyed the happiest time of his life in the months that he knew you. He wrote of the kindness of your parents welcoming him into your family, and his excitement about your plans for the future. He was a lovely lad. Taken too soon, but the good Lord, in his wisdom, had other plans.'

We arrive back at the farmhouse where Molly and two of her friends are setting out tables of food and drink for the wake. Sean's photo album is laid at one end of the table. Irish ballads play quietly in the background. People begin arriving, introducing themselves to me – it seems they are all Sean's cousins to some degree or another, and they all know almost as much about me as I do.

'You've a very special cat, so Sean told us. Could you remind me of the name? Ah yes, Zylch. I'm a cat lover myself. I don't suppose you've any photos of the wee creature?'

'He is very special indeed,' I reply. 'But so difficult to photograph. I'm afraid I don't have any to show you.'

I learn from one of the cousins that my hair is the color of a cornfield in the rising sun, my eyes the blue of where the sky meets the ocean, and my skin like the petals of a rose.

As time goes on the voices become louder, there's laughter and children chasing each other in and out of the house.

The numerous cousins have many tales to tell of Sean, as well as one that is 'not suitable for a young lady's ears, Donald!'

Liam, his old schoolfriend who is also a cousin says 'Do you recall, Jacky, when he said he and Alice had flown up into the sky?'

Jacky shouts with laughter and slaps his thigh. 'He was always inclined to fancifulness, was our Sean.'

I smile politely and change the color of my eyes from light blue to black. Both men stare, and blink, and when they look again my eyes are once again their natural color.

Liam frowns and scratches his head, Jackie stares at my eyes again. They walk away, whispering to each other. There's fancifulness for you, I smile to myself.

It's after midnight before the last visitors have left, and I volunteer to clear things away so Molly and Joe can sit and relax. My bodyclock is on Boston time and I'm wide awake. As they sit by the fire I cast them both a *Snooze* spell. Once their eyes are closed it takes no time with the help of a little magic to have everything tidied, washed and put away.

Although I'm longing to be back home, members of the family have made plans to entertain me the next day.

It's a whirlwind of a trip through the town, where it seems everybody we pass knew Sean, and knows me, and I feel like something of a celebrity when people ask to have their photos taken with me.

Out of a clear blue sky, without any warning, it starts to rain, heavy cold rain driven by a fierce wind.

'Come on now,' cries Donald, one of Sean's uncles, 'let's get ourselves inside.'

We splash through puddles to a noisy pub, that in the States we call a bar. I'm reminded of Decima's English pub near Cory's castle. I can't wait to tell her about it. Sean promised to bring me here, and in a way, he has. I'm here because of him.

After a busy day of Irish hospitality, I'm ready for a wee nip back at Joe and Molly's. I've been overwhelmed by the kindness and generosity of Sean's people, but jet lag has caught up with me.

Next morning, after breakfast I hand Molly a packet. 'These are Sean's things. I have kept a few photos for myself, and if you don't mind I would like to keep the crucifix he wore around his neck. All his musical material is here too, except for the two songs he recorded for me. They're on a memory stick, and I've sent it to a friend in the music industry, because they are very, very good and I think he'll be interested. I'll let you know what happens.'

'He'd have wanted you to have everything he had, Alice, you were his world. Take anything for yourself you'd like to keep.'

I slip the chain and crucifix around my neck, and thank them for all they've done for me and how welcome they've made me feel.

They ask what my plans are, and I reply that I'm going to take a little while to explore and that I'll find my own way.

'You will always be welcome here,' says Molly, giving me a hug. 'Take care, and let us know when you are back to your home.' She tucks a packet of sandwiches and a bottle of apple juice into my backpack and waves as I amble down the lane to the road. I stop once for a last long look at the house. I walk for an hour, then I sit on a bench and look up at the sky and say, 'Sean, I've done my very best, I hope it was what you would have wanted. I love you, and now I'm going home.'

I click the ***Brmstick*** app and cruise slowly for a while over the mountains and lakes, taking in the glorious Irish landscape. until I arrive at the Atlantic coast. Then I push to superspeed, arriving home five hours earlier than I left Ireland. It's still dark when I climb into bed, where Zylch is curled up on the pillow. He gives a sigh of pleasure and tucks into my neck, stroking my face with a little clawed finger, until I fall asleep.

36

One more cog in the wheel

Alice

'What do you think, Zylch?'

'Exactly,' he replies.

'Exactly what?'

'Exactly right.'

'So you think it will suit me then?'

'Exactly.'

I suppress a small sigh. As much as I adore him, Zylch can sometimes be rather annoying. No longer the small, ugly blob my mother dropped in my hands five years ago, but a unique silver-coated Screecher. His fur is soft and wavy, and at first glance, seeing him curled up on his favorite chair, or chasing bugs in the garden, you'd think he was a cat. We've agreed that is to be his public persona. He'll keep his shapeshifting capabilities for when they are needed rather than randomly transforming himself whenever I have visitors, which has caused me a few headaches in the past.

Perched next to me on the bathroom basin, he hums

and admires himself in the mirror, practicing new poses. I tickle his ears to get his full attention.

I release my hair so it falls back down to my waist.

'OK, then I'll have it cut this week. I think I'll go for a choppy bob.'

'Cool,' says Zylch, cupping his chin in his hands and tilting his head to one side.

The fact is that waist-length hair isn't practical for my new lifestyle. I study my face in the mirror. My features are no longer those of a naïve young woman, but of an assured 32-year-old businesswoman, a little sharper, more defined.

How that little flower shop has changed our lives since we opened. So much happened so fast. Sita's appearance and her Insta posts made us an overnight success.

When the floral tributes left for Sean on the sidewalk lasted for almost a month, their colors unfaded and scent undiminished, his death attracted State-wide interest. When a troll claimed that they must be artificial, the police came to tell us they must be removed. However, when they were examined and found to be real, things took a crazy turn. A rumor started that Sean was a saint, and it quickly became viral, with a website devoted to him. I hoped that up there among the stars, he was looking down and laughing.

Other florists in town alleged we were using banned chemicals to make the plants live for so long. State investigators became involved. Each plant was meticulously analyzed and examined, my mother's flower gardens and greenhouses were inspected, and no trace could be found of the use of any artificial growing methods.

When Astrid was questioned as to how she produced such extraordinary plants, she put it down to the Brent Flats atmosphere and her love of nature and nobody could prove otherwise.

Demand for our plants grew so fast that I bought an adjacent derelict three-storey building. I had it renovated, knocking through a doorway from the shop to give us more space. Astrid no longer breeds Screechers, much to the delight of my father. She has an outlet on the second floor where she sells her own natural skin care products, and *Salvheal* oil rebranded as *Blossoms Elixir*. She shares the space with a young male beautician who uses the products for facials, manicures and pedicures.

On the top floor we designed a gallery for local artists to exhibit and sell their works. My father's unique ceramic flowerpots and garden decorations are popular items.

Visitors to the gallery can sit and relax, sipping from one of the drinks I create using petals, herbs and a sprinkle of enchantment, inspired by Zylch's original idea. In a little over two years we'd created what Decima described as the Archer Empire.

It has never been my ambition to be anything other than a small family business, and we have resisted the idea of expanding further. What we have works perfectly for us. We earn enough to live comfortably. We are able to employ more people, giving work to six people with health conditions and impairments, some with physical issues, two with mental health challenges, who help with wrapping and deliveries. Downtown HBC is becoming a desirable area commercially, with old buildings being bought and renovated. With Gauld and his corrupt cronies gone, council funding has been poured into improving the roads and lighting, encouraging the growth of boutiques and health food restaurants. This part of town even has a name and Instagram site: The Boho Quarter.

I am proud of how my idea, first sparked off by Zylch's suggestion, has become a success. I'm still living in the barn conversion. It's a perfect location for Zylch to roam and for me to grow my herbs. One of the newest and most popular orders from the shop is for posies of wildflowers, which grow in abundance both in the fields here and on the Brent Flats. Astrid and I have a method for making them last longer than normal. We donate sales from these to local charities.

I'm feeling in a good place, although I still cannot shake off lingering feelings of guilt about Sean's death. He and Ramon had been especially close, both being from the same church, and I sometimes WhatsApp him. When I confessed that I still held myself responsible for Sean losing his life due to my carelessness, Ramon said:

'If he knew that, it would break his heart, Alice. He only lived to make you happy, and if he had to die a hundred times for you, he'd do it willingly. You were never responsible for his death. It was his destiny and nothing could have changed it. Be at peace now, for his sake. It's what he would want. Do that for him.'

His words did bring me comfort and made me accept I was just one cog in the wheel of Sean's fate.

37

Happy birthday

Alice

Today is my 33rd birthday. I'm not the wide-eyed girl who once worked as Decima's PA at the Tower. In those days if you had told me I would become a confident, successful businesswoman, I'd have laughed. But here I am. Much water has flowed beneath the bridge since those days of highs and lows, and I feel I've arrived where I am meant to be. I still have Sean's photo beside my bed, but the pain I felt at first has dulled. I can look back on our time together with a smile and be grateful for the love he brought into my life.

The men who attacked us on the Brent Flats were eventually caught and tried. They are serving sentences for their part, although nobody was ever charged with Sean's murder. Despite continued and intensive searches for Gauld, no trace has ever been found. The Screechers took care of that.

Ramon has become a huge star in Korea. His first film premiered in LA last year. He sent invitations to Decima,

Cory and me. We traveled together and were able to spend time with him in between his TV and public appearances.

Life in Korea has been good for him. He's fit and healthy, and a relaxed self-assurance has replaced his previous swagger. Women worldwide adore him, from schoolkids to grandmothers. He travels everywhere with the personal protection of four leather-clad Korean Ninjas who are as lethal as they are beautiful.

Keeping his promise to Decima when he left Hawk Bay City, he walked her on his arm along the red carpet to the premiere of his first film. He had once sworn to Decima that he would always love her, but seeing how she and Cory are in love, he wished them happiness and is dating a tiny Korean make-up artist, with Decima's blessing. When you see them together the chemistry is still strong, but they realize their time is over.

'Yes, Zylch,' I murmur, looking at my reflection in the mirror. 'What a long way we've all come in the last five years. Thanks to you I've survived many things, and thrived due to your help. Life is good.'

He jumps down from the basin and cartwheels out into the garden, singing 'la li la li la la', making me smile.

I'm out in the garden potting herbs for tomorrow's delivery, when my phone rings. I see Sita's face smiling at me.

'Hi Sita, how are you doing?'

'I'm doing just fine, and I'll be in HBC next week. I

know how busy you are, but is there any chance we could catch up one evening after work? Share our news. Haven't seen you for ages.'

Lovely Sita, once the wife of the man I loved, now a friend who played a major part in the success of the flower shop.

'That would be great. How about next Tuesday? We could go and have a bite at that new Italian restaurant?'

'I'll pick you up, shall I? '

'Sounds great. Can't wait.'

The woman I had long ago decided to hate has become one of my dearest friends. She's beautiful, kind, generous and fun and we meet whenever she's in town.

On Monday I take the plunge and have my hair chopped. It feels strange not to have it swinging around my face and getting in the way when I'm planting the herbs, and I'm looking forward to not having to spend ages brushing it. My neck feels rather exposed, but the style definitely suits me. The chopped off hair will go to making wigs for people who need them.

Decima drops into the flower shop later. 'Turn around,' she says, 'so I can see the back.'

'Hm, I must say it suits you, much better than when it straggled all over the place. Yes, I like it.' She runs her fingers through my bangs. 'See you've got a few gray hairs coming through. Never mind, nobody will notice. They only show if you look very closely.'

Decima is never going to be a diplomat.

She says it as she sees it and means no harm. Now she's settled with Cory, she's a different person. Out of all of us, she's changed the most. Still outspoken and opinionated but the anger has gone. That's true happiness for you right there.

I tease her about fussing with my looks when she barely bothers herself these days.

'You know what writers call this?' She twists around and pats her behind. 'Writer's butt. I wear it with pride.'

'And so you should.'

She's always been so passionate about reading, it shouldn't have come as a surprise when she took up writing. Her first novel, a romance set in an English castle at the time of the Plantagenets is due out next year. She sure has made the most of all the trips back to England to sort Cory's inheritance. When it finally came through, they moved out of town. Surprising us all by turning their backs on Decima's dream ranch in Santa Fe to settle way up north in Minnesota. When she discovered a whole community of Siberian Husky breeders around Antler Creek just west of Lake Superior, there was no stopping her. She fell in love with the place. Twinkle and Barney aren't pulling any winter sleds yet but I reckon it'll only be a matter of time. It's a new life for us all. When they come to town they stay at my parents house. They could stay next door with us, our place is much more spacious, but Decima says she feels truly at home with Patrick and Astrid. They refuse to get married. Decima says her writing deadlines have to come first. . I suspect time will change that. Meanwhile, we all go up to Antler Creek for Thanksgiving, as Decima's true found family.

This year we'll be meeting Cory's nephew, Jonty. After Decima's stories about his mother, Erica, that was a b – i – g surprise, but she reckons 100 acres is big enough for all of us.

I laugh. 'Thanks Decima, that's put my mind at rest.'

When I arrive home, Zylch is collecting wild flowers for the shop tomorrow. 'What a good boy you are, Zylch. You're so helpful.'

'Nice hair,' he says, eating a mouthful of flowers.

I wake up on Tuesday with a smile on my face, thinking how content I am with my life. I ruffle my new hairstyle, pleased with the way it falls naturally back into place.

Sita is waiting for me when the shop closes, and we walk down to the harbor for cocktails.

Sita has opened her first home in California for women escaping abusive relationships. 'Not just for Indian women,' she explains. 'It's there for anybody who needs it. Sadly there's already a huge demand, but we believe they will all get back on their feet eventually. The women are already coming up with ideas for supporting themselves and each other.'

She's glowing with pleasure as she talks about her plans, and then she turns and asks me 'What about you? Tell me everything.'

'There's not a lot to tell, nothing much has happened since we last met. I saw Ramon a while ago. Sharing the grief has definitely helped both of us, my feelings of guilt too, he's so reassuring and kind.

She squeezes my hand. 'I'm glad to hear that, Alice. It's been a long time. You've no need to torture yourself over that any more. Now, take me to this new find of yours.'

We link arms and stroll along the harborside to Dolce Vita. They've only just opened but already they're my new favorite restaurant in town. The bar is buzzing. I'm so pleased for them. They didn't hesitate to stock the flower syrups we sell in the shop. Not even on sale or return, they bought twenty on the spot. We are shown to high stools at the bar to wait for our table. As we sip our cocktails, I spot a few lined up on the back shelf, beautifully-lit with a mirrored background, and enjoy pointing them out to Sita.

We linger over the meal until she looks at her watch and sighs. 'Sorry, I've got a long day ahead tomorrow. Let's catch up again soon?'

'Sure. It's been a treat seeing you, as usual. It's my turn this time.'

I signal for the waiter, pay the bill.

Sita looks at her watch. 'I'd drive you home, Alice but...'

'Oh no! I wouldn't expect you to, Sita. I'm happy to stay a while. It's such a heavenly night.'

She grins widely. 'OK, if you're sure. See you next time,' she touches her cheek to mine and gives me a big squeezy hug.

I walk down to the harbor and lean against the wall, enjoying the reflections of the moonlight and stars dancing in the water.

People stroll pass, chatting, and I breathe in the salty air, drawing it down into my lungs and closing my eyes, living in the moment.

All of a sudden the hairs on the back of my neck stand up. The scent of cumin and coconut floats around me.

'You are even more beautiful than I remember, Alice.'

I turn away from the water to see Jai, smiling down at me. My heart explodes into a million butterflies. I have to hold the harbor wall behind me to steady myself.

'Jai? Why are you here?'

'I want to say something I was not free to say all that time so long ago. I've been working in Costa Rica for the last two years, and got back yesterday. Sita and I have always kept in touch. She told me she was meeting you here, and I've been watching you all evening. I couldn't take my eyes off you. I have missed you every moment since we last met. Every second of every minute, of every day, my heart has ached for you.'

'What do you want to say to me?'

'I want to tell you I loved you the first moment I saw you, before we'd even spoken a word. I have loved you ever since. I love you now, I will always love you and if you will have me, I will never leave you again.'

I'm speechless. I can do nothing but stand and stare at him.

'There is something I have waited such a very, very long time to do.'

He holds out his arms.

I lean into him and rest my head on his chest. He strokes my hair and puts his arms around me, holding me against his heart.

He lays his head on mine, and we stand there locked together, with only the quiet swishing of the water breaking the silence.

I feel if I could stand there like that forever, I'd ask nothing more of life.

'There is something I have to tell you,' I say. 'It's about my family.'

'I know about your family, you told me when we first met. Your mother is a sorceress who breeds Mottled Screechers. And I knew you were a witch that day by the harbor, when you helped the old lady who was mugged. I saw what you did then, and I knew.'

'And you don't mind?'

'What is there to mind? I would love you if you had a wart on your chin, wore a pointy hat and flew around on a broomstick.'

'Well, actually, since you mention it, I don't wear a pointy hat, but about the broomstick …'.

38

A special day

Alice

I wake up to a cold, misty morning. The leaves on the trees, and the petals on the flowers, are spotted with dew. Downstairs I can hear my mother Astrid, in her kitchen, rattling crockery. I wrap myself in a bathrobe and follow the aroma of coffee wafting up the stairs.

'I'm not sure it's worth all the messing around,' she says, handing me a mug. 'We've always been quite happy with instant coffee, and your father prefers it. I only get this machine out when Decima's coming.' The coffee machine was a gift from Decima.

She bites her lip and gestures to half a dozen outfits draped on hangers on the kitchen unit knobs. 'I really can't decide what to wear. Which do you think?'

'The pink one. It will go nicely with the roses. You'll look lovely.'

My father walks into the kitchen, pours a coffee from the machine, tips half into the sink and tops it with hot water and a dash of milk.

'Happy?' he says, putting his hands on my shoulders and looking into my eyes. 'Sure you're doing the right thing?'

'Absolutely certain,' I smile.

'So am I. I couldn't be happier for you.'

There's a knock on the door.

'Here they come!' shouts Astrid. 'They're here!'

A crowd of laughing women burst through the front door.

'If you want coffee, it's that way,' Decima appears at the bottom of the stairs and waves an arm at the kitchen door. 'We're using this room to get the bride ready.'

She pushes into the living room. 'You would NOT believe what used to go on in here,' she laughs.

Over the years since my mother and father cared for her after the fire, she has become almost one of the family, totally at ease here. 'It's the first home I ever had,' she tells everyone.

The women busy themselves preparing me for my big day.

Sita's gift to me is a sapphire blue silk saree threaded with silver, that she pleats and folds on my body over a matching bodice. Decima insists on doing my make-up. 'You've no idea,' she says. 'You never have had.' Despite my fears, she uses a light touch, bringing out the blue of my eyes and adding a subtle sparkle to my cheeks and lips. My hair has grown in the months since I had it cut, and Decima folds it into a neat pleat.

'That's perfect Decima,' says Lorelei who arrived yesterday and stayed with Decima overnight.

'It was a blast,' Lorelei says. 'We took to each other immediately and spent the whole evening recalling our battles and laughing over them. She is nothing like her TV personality. I really like her.'

By late morning the mist has lifted. The garden is at its most beautiful, decorated with raindrops sparkling like diamonds in the sun. Astrid's roses are in full bloom, perfuming the air.

My father knocks at the door. 'All ready?' he asks.

Sita, Decima, Shelley and Lorelei, my maids of honor lead the way, with Shelley's two girls scattering petals ahead of me. I hook my hand into Patrick's elbow and we tread slowly across the grass to where Jai stands beneath an arch of Zepherine roses, with his best man Cory.

My eyes are fixed on Jai. I notice touches of gray in his hair. We have waited so long for this day.

Shelley's husband James plays Sean's *Symphony of the Stars*, and *She's the One*. Scorpio's version has become a massive hit, reviving his career.. The sweet notes twirl in the air, bringing a lump to my throat.

Zylch trots at my side, his long fur shining like burnished steel. He wears a bow tie. He had to be persuaded not to transform into an elephant for Jai to ride on, and has settled for being the ring bearer.

When Jai slips the ring on my finger, and raises my

hand to his lips, tears balance on my eyelids for a few moments before they escape and begin to roll down my cheek. He wipes them tenderly away with his thumbs, and then he kisses me for the very first time.

Epilogue

The sea is calm today. Flat and silent and reaching endlessly to an invisible horizon. I wish I had a camera. I've sat here a long, long time, feeling the sun on my face, listening to kids yelling in the distance, burning these hours and minutes into my brain so I'll never lose them. It's an image that must last me a lifetime.

This is my last but one stop. I'm tired of being permanently on the move, sleeping with one eye open, listening for the click of a door handle, watching and listening for danger. Seven years of this is long enough.

What am I going to miss most? Instagram.

Following Ramon's career. Remembering how I used to laugh at him when he said he'd be a movie star, I smile wryly. Four blockbusters, a private plane, the world at his feet. Hollywood are offering megabucks, but he's happy with the Koreans. He bought his folks a nice place in Hawk Bay City and made his mother's dream come true when he set her up in a small restaurant serving Mexican dishes. His father gave up working at the docks and helps out in the restaurant. Chatting to customers mostly. The walls are decorated with posters of Ramon in his role as the Korean Zorro.

Alice finally got her man. The Alice I remember was a curvy, innocent girl, naive, timid and nursing a broken heart. She still has the big blue eyes, the golden hair, but that's where the similarity ends. She's confident, radiant, a businesswoman, wife and mother of twin girls. Somehow I'm not entirely surprised. I always felt there was more to her than we saw.

I watched her shop opening on TV, and the arrival of the Indian celebrity, the one Decima had hoped would break Alice live on TV. The memory of how I helped Decima there leaves a bitter taste. What a twist of fate that the two women became close friends. Like many others, I've been curious about Alice's plants and their almost magical longevity. Despite extensive investigations and laboratory examinations, they always come through as just plants. To give her more space to grow her plants, she and her husband bought two of the empty properties on the Brent Flats. They renovated one for their home, and turned the other into a center for environmental studies. It's like everything she touches turns to gold and I couldn't be happier for her. She deserves it.

Cory and Decima. Who'd have thought! But on the other hand, maybe it's not so strange. They're both Brits by origin and it could be that they give each other exactly what they both need and want. Stability, commitment, safety. Yeah, I can see how that works for them. The aristo was always in Cory. I should have guessed that one!

Sean? That hit me hard. He was a decent kid, didn't deserve to end up like that. Still, he left a great legacy. Two great musical hits and the revival of Scorpio's career.

OK, *She's the One* is a tad schmaltzy, but that *Symphony of the Stars* is truly one of the most magnificent pieces of music I ever heard. It brings tears to my eyes. A true classic. All royalties go towards an outfit in Ireland that improves the lives of youngsters. Maybe in a way it was better he went when he did, because Alice's heart was never going to be totally his.

So apart from Sean, everything worked out pretty well for the CGO TV crew, and you could say they owe it all to me. If it hadn't been for the destruction of the Tower, we'd likely still be churning out daytime TV programs, always seeking new angles.

It's funny how a few words can set off a chain of events.We got so close, Decima and I. Those times with just the two of us, relaxed, satisfied, not me worrying about competing with the youngsters. I was good for her. We were good for each other. She knew she could rely on me, I'd always take care of her. The ongoing battle with Lorelei, the problems with sponsors, you could see how it was dragging her down, wearing her out. Together we could have made a new life. Move out of Hawk Bay, get away from the rat race the TV station had become. We could have gone to Sante Fe, had a decent house, a bit of land and the dogs she'd always wanted. With her reputation she would grow her Insta followers even more, she's a natural influencer. I'd have been there to make sure she never failed to surprise. I was certain she'd jump at the idea when I put it to her. The age gap wasn't an issue. I thought it through for a while, until I felt we were close enough and it was the right time. We were sitting together on the sofa at her place, watching the sun going down. Each of us with a glass of red wine, some chips, slow background music playing, my arm around her, her head resting on my shoulder.

I said: 'I want you to come and live with me. We'll move to Santa Fe. Just the two of us.'

She knocked me back with a brutality that felt like a punch to the gut. The wine spurted out of her mouth onto the table, as she laughed and choked. She laughed until tears ran down her face, her shoulders heaving, slapping her hands on her thighs.

'Oh Josh! You crack me up.'

Just like that! She destroyed my dream. I laughed with her, pretending it was all a joke. But something inside me died.

Next day, I called Gauld. I'd been his CGO spokesman at the Tower for years, and lately he'd been confiding in me more and more. 'About your proposal. I'm in.'

He'd been on at me for months. He was into the Mafia for millions and they were running out of patience.

I didn't care about him, but how I reveled in the thought of seeing Decima's realm wrecked. The more I thought about it, the better I liked it. The $5 million Gauld would pay me would be a bonus.

It wasn't hard for me to get hold of the things I

needed and rig them up in place in Decima's office. Then all I had to do was to go to the basement late at night and push the right buttons. How could I have known she was up there? For all that I wanted to damage her, the last thing I wanted was to kill her. Or to kill anybody.

When I set up to trigger the fire, I had no idea how poorly-constructed the Tower was. Instead of wrecking just the top floor, the whole place went down, and people died. I was in shock. The whole thing became unreal. Like everyone else at first, I thought Decima was dead! Can you imagine my horror knowing what I'd done?

When I read they thought I died in the fire too, I decided to play along. I'd disappear, presumed dead. It was the safest option. The reports were saying that the heat of the fire was such that the three bodies were unidentifiable...

Investigations proved the fire was started deliberately. Law enforcement are still searching for the culprit. Once they are found, they'll be going away for life.

I disappeared, moving around, blending in, changing my appearance. I had enough money to keep going for a while, until Gauld coughed up, but he never did. He simply vanished and has never been found. I have no job, no money and am officially dead. That tenacious local reporter Tillman produced a Netflix documentary exposing just how evil Gauld was. I'd always known of his mob connections, but learning the full extent of his ruthless dealings shocked me. I was disgusted at having connived with him. I hope he's burning in hell.

One thing the documentary got wrong was that the fire at the Tower was Gauld's attempt to kill his adopted daughter, Decima, making her go into hiding, fearing for her life. That's wrong. The plan was only to get his hands on the insurance money, and like me, he had no idea Decima would be there when the fire started. He committed hundreds of heinous crimes, but that wasn't one of them. I think I'd like her to know that.

My kids believe I'm dead, and that really tears at my heart, but not as much as the pain I'm going to bring them. I've missed seeing my grandson grow up. I've killed three people. Those words go around and around in my head, day and night. I've killed three people. I've killed three people. All because Decima laughed at me.

All these years of living a lie have lost me everything, including my self-respect.

I walk back into town and stop outside the Sheriff's office. I take one more look around me, at daily life, and then walk in. A clerk looks up, says 'Can I help you?'

'Yes,' I reply. 'My name is Josh Harris, and I was responsible for the fire at the Tower in Hawk Bay City.

Dear Reader,

I hope you have enjoyed your time with Alice, Decima and the boys. This is the first novel I've ever written and it has been quite an experience. No need to try to imagine what everybody will do next – they decide and do it themselves, frequently waking me up during the night and interrupting at sometimes inconvenient moments to nudge me to write down their thoughts and deeds. I've come to love each of them, despite their faults .

I'm looking forward to finding out what the future holds for them all as their stories continue. If you would like to know too, do sign up to my mailing list (*http://eepurl.com/GKLiL*) and I'll keep you posted.

New authors and books rely so much on positive feedback, so if you have the time and the willingness, please do an Alice spell and cast a #review onto Amazon :)

May whatever you read always bring you joy,

Kelly

The Bewitched Trilogy
by Kelly Alleyn

1: The Tower of Secrets

A love triangle with a twist

Powerful, driven, TV presenter Decima is a wounded soul
with all the trappings of wealth and fame. She compensates
for her inner unhappiness by using her position to dominate
all who work for her. Alice, her naive, kind PA, has always
been an outsider because of her strange powers. She will need
to use them to stand up for herself if she is to survive in
Decima's world. When evil forces threaten, they must unite to
survive, as each strives to find love and security in a world of
danger.

2: *The Witch's Tale*

Dark forces align against Alice and her tormentor

Seemingly naive secret witch Alice is promoted to TV chat show co-presenter alongside ruthless, manipulative Decima. As Alice's self-confidence grows, so too does the TV crew's passion for her and she becomes the unwitting target for Decima's bitter jealousy. But Alice's magical powers are a good match for Decima's dirty tricks, and she uses them in ways that leave Decima increasingly bewildered. Away from the studio, there are momentous changes in Alice's personal life whilst Decima finds the true meaning of love in an unlikely place. As their silent skirmish continues, dark forces capable of destroying them both align. When the world as they know it crumbles around them, an evening of terror leads to a dramatic twist of fate.

3: Twists of Fate

A bombshell confession reveals the Tower's final secret

Through the highs and lows of love and loss, hope and fear, it takes a touch of magic to bring Alice and Decima the true happiness they seek. In a shocking final twist, the Tower's biggest secret is unveiled.

Twitter @KAlleynWriter

TikTok @kellyalleyn

Facebook Kelly Alleyn Page: bit.ly/443sLRm

www.ingramcontent.com/pod-product-compliance
Lightning Source LLC
Chambersburg PA
CBHW031259120726
47906CB00003B/809